SECRETS

OF

THE

DEAD

SECRETS OF THE DEAD

SIMBI FEYISARA

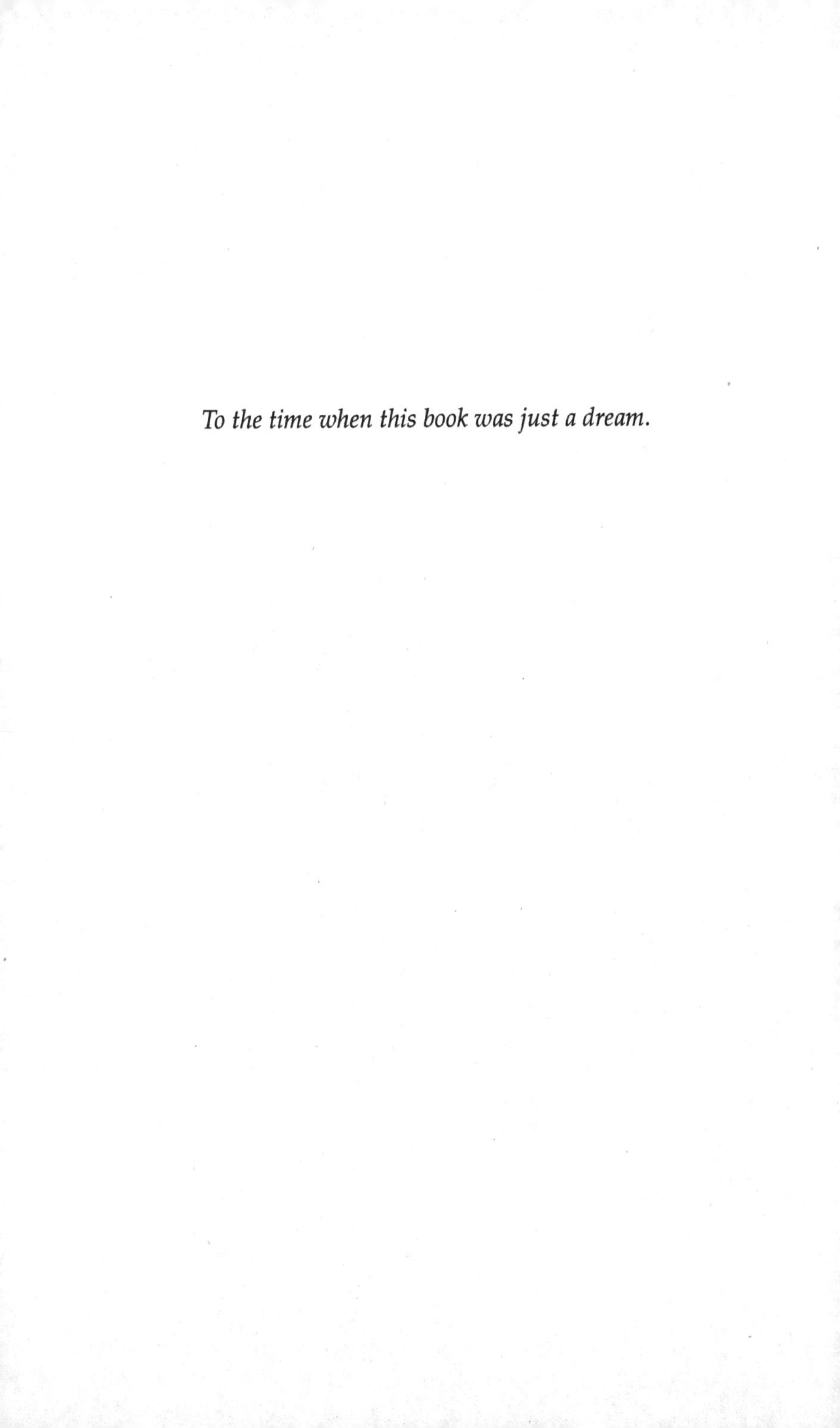

To the time when this book was just a dream.

ONE

Behind every door in The Bells lay a secret. They possessed an undeniable weight, an invisible burden carried by my dorm mates. And for me, they were a currency and one of the many reasons I always got what I wanted.

Everyone else waited for Vivienne Marks to solve their problems. She was rich and popular and always had time for people—even me. But if I wanted something, I took it. It had started small, with a hair clip, then led to perfume and clothes. Once Vivi realized her things were going missing, she'd stopped getting the good stuff. That had worked well for the remnants of my conscience, because it was not stealing if it was cheap.

My curtains were drawn, but light flooded into the dorm room from Vivi's bedside window. It shimmered across the gray floorboards, Vivi's open closet, and her desk crammed with creams and powders. The sunrays tried to stretch, thinning and dying as they reached my half of the room.

I lay on my side, propped up on my elbow. My gaze tracked Vivi as she rolled up clothes.

She paused and looked over her shoulder, outgrown brown highlights disappearing behind her back as she turned to face at me. "It's the last day before the holidays. Don't you have anything better to do than watch me pack?"

"No. I've always enjoyed window-shopping."

She groaned then stuffed a rolled-up sweater into her designer suitcase and zipped it, the expanding seams struggling to hold the case together. It was hard to believe we were only going away for two nights. She walked to her desk, pulled out a drawer, and searched through a bag of padlocks and keys.

I frowned. "Why are you bringing a lock with you to the lodge?"

She turned her back to me. "Because we are sharing rooms. And I don't trust you."

Good point.

"And I thought these last few months had been going well?" I deadpanned.

Vivi turned, raising a brow.

I couldn't quite work her out. Unlike the other girls, who didn't hide their blatant disdain, Vivi didn't overtly display it. She didn't know everything I had done, but she knew enough. Yet, when I invited myself on her trip to the lodge, she didn't protest. At first, I thought she was either a really forgiving person or too rich to care. But the mask was slipping.

She fumbled with another padlock, jerking the key inside.

"Do you trust the rest of them?" I tipped my head to the

door, beyond which were the rest of our housemates. Vivi had good reason to hate each of them, yet she had organized a trip to spend two nights at Brittles Cove with them to bond.

Vivi blew out a breath and threw down the key. "Of course. They are my friends."

It was subtle, but her tone was different, as though she didn't believe the words herself. She leaned over her desk, pulled out a drawer, and placed the padlock inside before opening small boxes.

I still hadn't packed. I was waiting to see if the horror on the girls' faces when they found out I was coming would be satisfying enough.

"Where is it?" Vivi banged on her desk. She extended her hand, face reddening.

I pursed my lips. In situations like these, it was best to keep quiet. She could have been referring to hundreds of different things I had taken.

"Dani." She jerked her hand. "I'm not in the mood for one of your games. Where is my bracelet?"

My shoulders relaxed, and my eyes fell to her wrist. Vivi was rarely without the bracelet her Japanese grandmother had gifted her. Seven clunky charms hung off the gold, and while I may have been a thief and maybe a liar, I had taste.

I puffed out my chest, my voice carrying an unfamiliar conviction. "I haven't touched your bracelet."

She sighed, rummaging through her jewelry box with her name in silver embroidery down the side. She emptied earrings, necklaces, and rings onto the desk. I didn't stop her as she rounded the room to my side and pulled out my desk drawer, which was empty in comparison to Vivi's. She pulled out scraps of paper and old receipts before moving to another drawer and holding up a beige tub of face cream I had taken, meant to achieve radiant skin. It hadn't worked, and I had forgotten to return it.

I held back a laugh. "I said I didn't take your *bracelet*."

She tossed the tub back, jaw tense as she slammed the drawer shut. "I don't understand why you keep pushing. I am always trying to help you. Why are you so desperate to throw it back in my face?"

I swallowed. The moment someone knew they had something you wanted, they had power. Vivi probably would have given me half the things I'd taken, but everything came at a price.

I gritted my teeth. "I said I don't have it."

Vivi opened her mouth.

A knock at the door interrupted whatever she was about to say. She squeezed her eyes shut and exhaled sharply. "It's open."

At this, bright-ginger curls poked through the door. The accompanying face flashed a smile before her lips fell into an uncharacteristic frown. Mabel was the only one of our roommates who seemed not to have let The Bells crush her spirit. "Vivi." Mabel's forehead creased. "There's someone out here looking for you."

Vivi drew her head back. "Who?"

Mabel shrugged. "He said his name is Luke. Harper's trying to get rid of him, but he says he won't leave until he speaks to you."

I sat up straight, my interest piqued.

Vivi hesitated for a moment, pinching the skin of her

throat before she nodded. Mabel pushed open the door and turned to lead the way.

Vivi took slow steps behind, wiping her palms, then squeezed her hands tightly, and I followed.

If there was one thing that could unite the girls from The Bells, it was drama. Candice, a more tolerable housemate, leaned against the lobby doorframe, her hand in the pocket of her wide-cut jeans. Her rolled-up shirtsleeves revealed a stack of colorful braided bracelets.

"What's going on?" I slowed, hanging back as Mabel and Vivi entered the lobby.

Candice turned to face me, the silver stud in her eyebrow catching the light. Last week, there had been three piercings on her face, and now I was sure I counted four.

She nodded at Vivi. "Her boyfriend wants her back."

"Boyfriend?" I'd made a habit of knowing everything about the people around me. And I'd shared a room with Vivi for months, but there had been no mention of a boyfriend.

I peered into the lobby. Plush armchairs framed the walls—three painted white and one paneled in chestnut brown. A bulletin board hung on the side, normally pinned with the cleaning rota, part-time work opportunities, and the semester timetable. Now it held a poster featuring a shimmering silver dress. *Stylies* was written over it in a bold font. The welcome mat was askew, and Harper, my least favorite housemate, was blocking a pale-faced boy from entering The Bells.

Vivi approached, and the blood seemed to drain from his face. He was tall and thin with dark hair, the type who

seemed too easily intimidated to help me out of the predica-
ment that was my four-year relationship.

Harper stepped aside to let Vivi pass.

"Vivi," Luke said breathlessly. His cheeks rose as he
reached out a hand.

Vivi stepped back, hugging herself, hiding a trembling
hand. "Who are you?"

His mouth dropped open. "Please don't be like this.
Whatever I've done, I'm sorry. I still love you."

Vivi spluttered, struggling to find words. Then Harper
was between them. She had outgrown her famous bob, and
her hair, a few shades lighter, dangled down her back. "She
doesn't want to talk to you."

Harper barely made it to his chest. Luke didn't bother to
sidestep as he reached out again to Vivi. "I promise we can
make it work. Let's talk somewhere private."

"Luke." Harper thrusted a hand into his chest.

He staggered backward.

My stomach clenched. A glint of gold caught my eye
from Harper's wrist. Her sleeves slid back, revealing a
familiar set of dangling charms. She jerked the material
back over her hands, her eyes wide.

Vivi didn't see. It was not often I was falsely accused. I
could have exposed her right then. But there was something about keeping secrets, knowing truths others
wanted to hide, and seeing how far they would go to
protect them.

"I'm not going to say it again." Harper gestured to the
exit, nodding. "Go."

Luke shook his head. "Not until I hear it from you,
Vivi."

Vivi scoffed. "Go," she echoed with a half laugh. "I don't even know who you are."

I could almost see the moment his heart broke. His face fell, his eyes laced with tears, before he turned and left The Bells.

Good for him. Nothing good ever happened here.

Harper trailed him as he walked down the steps, then she returned, slamming the door behind her.

Mabel pouted. "Poor thing. Are you sure you've never seen him before?"

Vivi shook her head. "Never."

Harper carefully placed an arm over Vivi's shoulder. "That's so weird."

Candice and I stepped back as Harper guided Vivi out of the lobby and through to the hallway.

"He seemed like he really knew you," Mabel said wistfully, following behind them.

"Yeah," Vivi agreed, her hand pinching the skin of her neck. Their voices grew quiet as they walked away.

I looked out the lobby window. Luke sat on the bench outside, head in his hands.

"What do you think that was about?" Candice asked, leaning back into the doorframe.

I shrugged. "No idea."

"Liar. You always know what's going on."

I didn't. But it was important for people to think I did. I pursed my lips as I straightened my back and walked to my dorm room.

Vivi sat on the edge of her bed.

Harper leaned toward her from a desk chair. "Just leave it. If he comes back, we will deal with it together."

Vivi nodded.

"Sounds like he was catfished," I said. "He's cute. There could have been something there. It's hard enough for someone to love you when they know you. He has managed to fall in love without meeting you."

Vivi cocked her head. "Shouldn't you be packing?"

"It's only two nights, and I pack light."

"Wait. What?" Harper scowled. "She's coming?"

"Yes," I said. "I'm looking forward to it."

Harper blew out air. "You don't need to take pity on her."

"I can hear you," I said.

Harper rolled her eyes. "Vivi." She got up and stepped over Vivi's suitcase. "If you need anything, just let me know." Her shoulder brushed against mine as she passed, and she clicked the door shut behind her.

Vivi slumped forward. "Don't you ever think maybe it would be a good idea to make friends with the people you live with?"

"No."

Vivi scoffed. "But you're okay with coming away with us for the weekend?"

My lips ticked up. "Sounds like fun. Being in the middle of nowhere with people who pretend they don't hate each other."

"I don't hate any of you."

"Really? Every single person out there is jealous of you."

"And you're not?"

"No." I shook my head. "I see what it's like for you. The pressure you're under."

Vivi didn't meet my eyes. "I think you're under more pressure than me. Trying to keep up with this pretense."

I waved my wrist for her to continue.

"Like you're okay being alone. Wouldn't it be nice to have friends?"

"I don't need anyone else."

She swallowed. "I won't give up on you."

Something sank in my stomach. She always looked for some goodness that wasn't there. Most of the girls didn't bother with the small talk and quickly blamed me as soon as anything went wrong. Despite everything I had done to Vivi, she wanted to see past it. I braced myself, ready to lash out to prove her wrong.

There was no redemption. She was wrong to trust me.

But she lowered herself to the floor, crouched by her suitcase, and returned to her packing. Her back was to me, shielding the contents, but I could see her. The mirror above offered the perfect view of furrowed brows and a sweat-lined forehead as she slipped one final object into her bag. A knife.

TWO

I didn't move. It felt binding. My skin tightened at the arm around my shoulder. The thick build leaned into me. The touch meant to be a gentle embrace weighed heavy. With guilt? Disgust?

My eyes wandered across the sandy-brown-and-white walls of the common room that had seen so much. Boxes labeled "Stylies" in glitter ink were stacked on the pool table. Beanbags in every color of the rainbow lined the wall at the back. The yellow was stained red from one of the many parties thrown at The Bells. Three nude sofas framed a long oak coffee table with one leg propped up by folded paper. The TV murmured in the background, but my mind kept drifting to thoughts of Vivi and the knife.

Jamie swept back his straw-like hair and tapped lightly on my forehead. "What's going on in there?"

He had been my constant for the past four years. At one point, I might have loved him, but now, he was causing problems and running out of use. I didn't always have an issue, but there were some things I didn't want to ruin my reputation. He was reckless, known for his run-ins with the police, and lately, I didn't know if I could trust him with the truth.

He withdrew his arm from my shoulder, and air flowed freely into my lungs.

I shrugged. "I was just thinking about swim practice. Our captaincy election is coming up soon."

Most girls on the swim team didn't like me, and while Grace, our captain, recognized they needed me, not everyone cared.

His narrow nose wrinkled. "It doesn't matter who is captain. You're always going to be the best on that team. Actually." He turned, clasping my hands in his. "I was thinking."

Always dangerous.

"Even though we both live on campus, sometimes I feel like it's still hard for you to find time to see me."

It had been one of my subtle clues. I was glad he was finally picking up on them. I thought I had been too harsh by volunteering to spend two nights away with my housemates.

"It's not like how it was back home. Your stupid family aren't around."

I flinched.

"And I know how much you hate it at The Bells. So I think we should move in together next year."

I wet my lips and tried to keep my face neutral. "Now, that's an idea."

He exhaled. "I thought you might say no."

I didn't say yes.

"I know your parents still aren't happy with us," he continued.

That was an understatement. They had hoped that we would grow out of our relationship. I couldn't get through a phone call without them asking why I was ruining my life by choosing Jamie. But lately it didn't feel like a choice. Wherever I went, he followed. He wasn't planning on going to college, and I was going to give it a couple of months before I blamed the distance for our breakup. I'd thought I was finally free of him until he dropped me off at Stedmond College and told me he had also managed to get in.

"Some of your stuff is already at mine. And it's a studio, so it would just be us. You won't have to worry about anyone else."

I stared down at my lap. "I'll think about it."

"Dani." Mabel's head popped into the common room, a bright smile on her face. The only other body part visible was the hand she waved at Jamie. I could never match her energy. It was unnerving. "I hear you're coming with us to the lodge."

"Yeah." I nodded.

Mabel beamed. "Great, we're going to have so much fun."

Jamie stared through the door as Mabel disappeared. "What's wrong with her?"

"What do you mean?"

"She was nice. To you."

I shrugged. "I guess I'm not all bad."

"And you like her?" he teased.

"She's cool. I feel a little sorry for her. She got in on a

scholarship, and it's been canceled. She doesn't know how she will make it through next year."

Jamie's brows rose. "Really? That sucks."

I hummed. "I should go."

He leaned in, and I shot up. "I'm going to be late for practice." I took hesitant steps then tried to mask the awkward moment, offering him a smile. I walked away, my body tense.

"Dani," he called, "are we okay?"

My smile didn't falter, but everything was becoming harder to fake. "We're fine. I'll see you later."

I rushed back into the dorm room. Vivi's packed suitcase was under her desk, a jacket and handbag perched on top. I paused momentarily, something telling me to go for the knife, but I grabbed my gym bag instead. It was the last practice before the holidays, and of course, I was late. I closed the door behind me and trudged through the hallway, only stopping when I heard voices in the common room.

The TV was off, but Jamie was still there at the edge of the sofa, with Mabel next to him. My first hope was that he was cheating—a good excuse for an easy way out of this pathetic relationship. Then Mabel turned, her eyes red and teary.

I stepped into the room. "Everything okay?"

Mabel smoothed her hand along her skirt and rose. "Yeah. I'm sorry." She wiped tears from her cheeks. "You guys are really kind. Jamie was trying to help."

"With what?"

Mabel swallowed.

"Advice," Jamie said. "My cousin got into college on a

scholarship. As long as she passes this year, there are loads of things she can do."

Mabel nodded. She started to speak but thought better of it. Her throat worked as she walked toward me. She gave me a light touch on the shoulder before leaving.

I tilted my head in question.

Jamie held out his hands, his lips curling into a smirk. "What?"

"Why was she crying?"

"A lot is riding on this for her. She's overwhelmed. It's good she has people around her for support." He leaned forward and sipped water from a glass.

I didn't believe him. Usually, he was an open book. It was me who kept the secrets. "Are you sure that's all?"

Now he was full-on grinning. "It's been a long time since I've seen a jealous side to you."

I bit back my laughter. "Not jealous. Curious."

He leaned back into the chair.

I was leaving. He had no business at The Bells.

"You're going to be late to practice. Try not to be too much trouble." He winked.

I clenched my jaw. "See you later."

I breathed in the strong smell of chlorine welcoming me back into my element. Stedmond's crest lay at the bottom of the pool in the form of a mural, distorted by sloshing water and bobbing heads. Coach leaned forward from a plastic chair. The back of her silver hair gleamed, and her cheers filled the space.

"You're late." Steph scowled. She pressed her hand into her side. A red swimsuit framed her tall, slender figure. "You're so lucky I'm not captain. I'd have you kicked off the team."

"You wanting to get rid of the best swimmer is exactly why you shouldn't be captain."

"We work as a team." Steph scoffed, blocking my path as I tried to sidestep her, and water dripped from the two braids of her coily hair. "No one cares how good you are. Wanting you off the team is exactly why I will become captain. It's one of my pledges."

Something in my chest tightened. "You can't do that."

"No." She shook her head, and water snaked down her neck. "But I can make it unbearable enough that you'll quit. You can come to training, but you can forget about participating in any swim meets." She leaned in. "There are a few people who still think you should be on the team, but we've been waiting for you for the past ten minutes. You don't respect our time. You're still standing here talking to me."

I shoved her out of the way, ignoring the heat of stares and an awkward wave from Diane as I continued my walk of shame past the pool and through to the changing rooms. My lateness wasn't a rare occurrence, but now that Steph was whispering in everyone's ears, they all seemed to notice.

There was nowhere better for me than the water. That was the one thing I wasn't willing to lose.

I changed in record time and walked to the pool with a point to prove.

Coach folded her arms across her blue-and-white tracksuit. Her slicked-back hair was unmoving as she shook her head. "Dani."

I bit my lip. "I know."

She took a deep breath. "Insanity. That's what it's called when you keep doing the same thing despite getting the same results, and if your behavior isn't going to change, then it's me who has to do something different."

I swallowed the lump in my throat. The pressure eased as I entered the water. No one spoke to me as we worked through drills. They only acknowledged me when we lined up for the final race. Sometimes, I would let someone else win. Coach suspected, but she never called me out. The girls were smug when they won. They celebrated with thrusted chests and long, hard stares as though beating me was a prize in itself.

I didn't need to say anything. I would keep it to myself that I gave them their greatest achievement, and at any given moment, I could bring them straight back down to earth. Like today.

I pushed myself, putting everything into my strides, taking quick breaths as my head broke through the water's surface then plunged again. My arm sliced, my heart pounded, and my feet flexed. Today, there was no one close.

"Well done, Dani. You almost broke your record," Coach said.

None of the girls seemed to share her joy. Only Kelly, a short, burly girl, offered a pat on the back before climbing out of the pool and standing with the rest of the team.

We wrapped towels around ourselves and waited for Coach to speak.

She stepped forward, notepad in hand. "Ladies, we

have one more thing to discuss. Grace has been an admirable captain for almost three years, and as this is her final year, we will be voting for a replacement as team captain. You will have next semester to learn the ropes from Grace herself before you are expected to lead the team next year. We have three people who have expressed their interest in running. Steph, Diane, and Lucy."

My jaw clenched. Steph had had no shot at becoming captain until I'd become her main campaign pledge. The only one who didn't hate me was Diane. If anyone else was captain, I was in trouble.

"They have all put together their pledges," Coach said. "Look on your Atlas profiles to have a read and cast your votes."

Steph stepped forward. Red braces on her teeth flashed as she said, "You can always come and speak to me directly. There are some things I would like to introduce that wouldn't fit on my campaign page."

My cheeks burned. I clasped my hands behind my back. Anger bubbled in my stomach. I zoned out as Diane and Lucy gave speeches then hung back as the girls approached the changing room. "Coach?"

"Dani?" She sighed. "What is it this time?"

"It's about the race for captaincy."

Her eyes widened. "You're thinking of running?"

I rolled my eyes. "You could at least hide your disbelief."

Coach smiled. "What about it?"

I wasn't stupid enough to believe I could become captain, but I was spiteful enough to ensure Steph didn't.

"Steph has been telling the girls that if she wins, she will cut me from the team."

Coach tipped her head back and laughed. "Is it working?"

I bit my lip. "Yes."

"Then maybe you need to think about how you can make good with the rest of your teammates. I can't do anything about Steph's campaigning techniques."

"You can tell her she won't be able to go through with it."

"Dani, you are one of our best swimmers, but you need to cool down. They are a team. If your behavior interferes and they don't think they can work with you, there's nothing I can do."

"You can kick her off the team."

"The same thing she is trying to do to you?"

"I am the better swimmer."

"Modest too." She placed a hand on my shoulder. "As long as she doesn't do anything to harm you physically, I can't get involved. If people are willing to vote for Steph to get rid of you, I'm sure there is a lesson for you to learn there."

She's right. There was a lesson there.

THREE

It was easy to tell when someone was lying. Everyone had their tells, and right now, Mabel was full of them. Her hands flexed and unflexed by her sides until she knotted them together behind her back.

"Um." Her eyes darted around The Bells parking lot. We were the only ones there, but she looked everywhere but at me. "I was just clearing out my car so there was space for all our things." She gestured to her beat-up blue car three rows back. "Thanks for mentioning my situation to Jamie. He really thinks I can get another scholarship." She fell into step beside me as I walked up the front steps of The Bells. "Do you remember the code for this week?"

I shook my head. The code to enter the building changed weekly. It was meant to allow cleaners into the communal areas, but it was mostly shared every time Tessa, our housemate, wanted to throw a party.

Mabel pulled out her cell phone and opened her email. Hands shaking, she pushed in the four-digit code. The door swung open, and she took one step into the lobby before faltering and holding up her cell phone. "Look."

I swept my hair back, still damp from practice, and leaned in. She showed me a message from a number I recognized as Jamie's.

"This is the scholarship his cousin did." She gripped the cell phone with two hands to steady herself. "The Leavy scholarship fund."

I moved back. It checked out.

"I don't have anything else to fall back on." She sniffed. "This could be it for me."

"And that's all you were talking about?"

She pinched her lips together—another tell—and said under her breath, "Yes."

A lie. It should have bothered me more, but Mabel wasn't a threat. "I hope it works out," I offered before walking through the lobby. "This place wouldn't be the same without you."

She straightened, and her cheeks flushed red.

Mabel followed as I stepped into the hallway, and the overhead lights lit up, illuminating her bright smile. She linked her arm through mine, and I resisted the urge to flinch.

"Why can't you be the way you are with me with the other girls?"

I pulled my arm away. "How is that?"

She drew her head back, as though searching for the right words. "Nice."

Something tightened in my chest. The sound of wheels scraping along the floor filled the corridor, saving me from answering.

"I'm dropping this in my car." Vivi approached in a bright-red jacket, pulling her suitcase behind her. "We are going to meet in the common room to plan before we go."

I rolled my eyes. "Really?"

Vivi shrugged and muttered, "It was Mabel's idea."

"It's always good to have a plan." Mabel beamed. "I'm going to get my things." She turned right into her dorm room, leaving me alone in the hallway.

I still had to pack. I should have gone straight to my dorm, but as I moved through the hallway, harsh, low tones issued from the common room.

I stopped and moved closer until I could make out the voices.

"I don't want to know what it's for," Candice said in her usual drawl. "And I didn't give you this. If Vivi—"

"We don't need to talk about this," Harper snapped.

I edged toward the entrance of the common room until the two girls came into view. Candice ruffled through her backpack. Braided bracelets slid down her arm as she handed over a rolled-up paper bag.

Harper snatched it. "Don't bring this up again."

I stepped into view. "What was that?"

Candice jumped. Her eyes darted from me to the paper bag now hidden in Harper's pocket.

Harper rolled her eyes. "I get allergies. Candice was kind enough to get me some tablets before we go to the lodge."

I cocked my head. "Do you think I'm dumb enough to believe that?"

Harper straightened. "Do you think I care?"

"Candice?" I asked.

Candice raised her palms. "I'm not getting involved in whatever this is."

Harper waved a hand. "Candice is not coming on the trip. In fact, she was just leaving."

Normally, Candice wasn't one to be dismissed, but she grabbed her backpack, refusing to meet my eyes as she left.

Harper's brows furrowed. She swiped at her forehead, reaching for strands that weren't there, then smoothed down her hair. The tips were dyed brown, similar to Vivi's style at the beginning of the year.

"Are you growing out your hair?" I asked.

"No, my hairdresser is busy. I'm not like you. I don't just go to anybody."

"Not busy enough to dye it?"

Harper rolled her eyes. "What do you want?"

"I think you owe me an explanation. Vivi accused me of stealing her bracelet."

She looked up. "I wouldn't put it past you. We can't trust you with anything." She rolled up her sleeves slowly and deliberately, revealing her bare wrists.

A laugh bubbled in my throat. I could still tell Vivi, but there was a chance she wouldn't believe me. This wasn't the first time one of the girls had stolen from her. I knew better than to rush in. I just had to wait until I was able to prove it.

I walked into the common room. Steph, Harper, and Vivi were already sitting on the sofa, surrounded by luggage.

Cropped bleached-blond hair styled in finger waves peeked from behind a wide handheld mirror. Tessa lowered it and leaned back into a red beanbag, watching me enter the room.

I dropped my bag onto the coffee table.

Steph glared. "No." She looked to Vivi. "It's bad enough I have to train with her. She is not coming to ruin this."

Vivi sighed. "Everyone is invited. And she isn't coming to cause trouble."

Steph held out her arms, swiveling her head. "Does anyone else want her here?"

"Steph, leave it." Harper rubbed her neck. "If this is what Vivi wants…" She trailed off, and Steph seemed to understand, slumping back into her seat.

"I've emptied out my car," Maria, the last of our roommates, said as she walked into the common room. Her curls were brushed back into a high ponytail that stretched her tan skin. She did a double take when she saw me but said nothing as she took a seat on the sofa.

In silence, we all waited for Mabel, the tension palpable. Backpacks rustled on laps as they checked nothing was missing. Everyone was dressed in layers, sweatpants, cardigans, and jackets. Everyone apart from Tessa. She tapped her six-inch heels on the ground and stroked freshly manicured nails over the beads of her glittery jumpsuit. I recognized the outfit. It was the same one she had worn on the billboards for Stylies, the clothing business she'd created. She had her eyes set on world domination by making everyone wear sparkles. She bought cheap clothes, slapped her logo on them, and sold them for triple their worth.

Tessa managed to convince Vivi about the idea, and she provided the financial support.

Harper, Steph, Maria, and Tessa developed the designs and marketing ideas. I had never been invited to their various business meetings, but I knew enough to know things hadn't been going well. Vivi had high hopes to add to her family's business portfolio, but I noticed when the adverts started disappearing, and now Vivi never spoke about it. She didn't have to. Tessa was always a walking advertisement reminding Vivi that while she may have been happy to walk away from the failing project, the rest of the girls needed it.

At first, it had worked. They'd made money. Then they'd lost it. Harper would say they'd spent more on advertising than they profited. Vivi would say they'd tried to scale too soon. If they asked me—and no one ever did—I would tell them the truth. The money was gone because one of them had stolen it.

Steph cleared her throat. "Now that we are all together, I think we should make a plan for Stylies."

The room stilled. All eyes snapped to Vivi's.

Her jaw tensed. "I think we should just try to enjoy this trip."

Tessa sighed. "We have put a lot into this business. We would enjoy it more if we knew what was happening."

"Hey, guys." Mabel stumbled into the room, arms filled with bags.

Harper bit her lip. They had been trying to get Vivi to talk about it for weeks. The moment was gone, but I knew we hadn't heard the last of it.

Mabel laid her bags on the table. "I am excited to spend

some time with you outside The Bells. I know we are going to have so much fun and to keep us busy." She emptied the bags, and board games clattered onto the table—Monopoly, Uno, and a pack of cards.

"Ugh." Tessa groaned. "Really, Mabel?"

"I've already made plans to watch paint dry," I muttered.

"Dani," Mabel said, "I have a sneaking suspicion you will end this trip liking a few of us."

I had spent almost a year in the same dorm with them and found them barely tolerable. This trip wasn't going to change much.

Heads turned as soft knocks sounded on the door.

"Hey," Candice said, a pitying look on her face. "Alex is here."

The room ran cold. We knew what it meant. Gazes lowered to the floor, and Mabel's face dropped. "Okay." She took a sharp breath and nodded. "Okay," she repeated under her breath.

Alex was Mabel's best friend, and she had been trying to get him clean for months. We often found him asleep in the common room or outside The Bells, shaking and eyes bloodshot. Mabel would go to calm him down. I didn't have to see him to know what condition he was in. The effect on Mabel told it all. She wasn't the one taking drugs, but addiction gripped her too.

"I'm so sorry to miss out." She swung a small backpack over her shoulder. "I need to stay with Alex and make sure he's okay. Um…" The coffee table clattered as she dragged her suitcase. "I want you all to take these games. This will be a perfect bonding experience for you all."

"Thank you, Mabel." Vivi smiled then added quietly, "I hope he's okay."

"Yeah," Mabel whispered to herself. She lifted her suitcase by the handle and followed Candice out of the room.

"Right." Tessa smirked. "So, we all agree we are telling Mabel we accidentally left the games behind? Or that there wasn't enough space in the car? Which could be true because that's one car gone, and I sold my car, remember?" Tessa cocked her head.

The girls stiffened. Somehow, they were back to Stylies already.

I sighed. "It's not Vivi's fault your business plans failed."

Tessa squeezed her eyes shut before opening them again. "No, but it's up to her whether or not we can try again."

"We don't have to talk about that right now," Vivi said, her voice strained and unnatural.

"We have to talk about it eventually," Steph said. "Some of us relied on that extra income to get through next year. I don't want to have to work odd shifts washing pots on the weekends. I know for you it isn't a problem."

Vivi lowered her head. Tension was heavy in the air as the girls' eyes pinned her. They were vultures, and Vivi was weak. I knew she would break. People only valued her for the things she offered. She might have considered me in the same way, but I got all the benefits without pretending to be her friend.

Vivi wrung her hands. "I'll think about it."

Tessa shook her head.

"I promise," Vivi added.

This wasn't enough. The girls shifted in their seats.

"I just need to talk to my parents. They will ask questions if I suddenly move so much money."

It was scary to watch. Shoulders relaxed, and smiles fixed in place.

The familiar splutter of Mabel's car went off in the parking lot, and the sound resounded around the room. It was always easy to tell when she was coming and going. The groan of the engine followed, and Vivi stood up. "Some of you can come in my car. Anyone else would be with Maria."

"I'm with Vivi," I called before anyone else could say anything.

Harper uncrossed her legs. "It's just you two, then. You will have to take some of our luggage so there's space."

I chewed my cheek. "You would rather that than spend a few hours in a car with me?"

Steph scoffed. "Yes."

I shrugged. "I don't mind. It's a long drive. I'll get to fill Vivi in on a few things."

Eyes flashed white. Jaws tensed.

Good. They remembered. I knew things about them, things they were desperate to keep from Vivi, and during such a long drive, anything could slip.

FOUR

Vivi lowered the radio volume, and the crunch of leaves and slow breaths filled the silence. Branches clawed at the car as we traveled a dark, winding path. The sound of the metallic scrape dragged along the roof.

Vivi winced, biting her lip as she leaned forward, her head directly above the steering wheel. "I'm sure it's up here somewhere," she said for a third time as we crept up the fifth route we had taken.

I looked back out the rear window. Maria's car had trailed us for miles, but now it was nowhere to be seen in the black. I knew better than to get my hopes up and wish for a tragic accident.

I sank into my seat. The knife was on my mind again. I hadn't mentioned it. The more I thought about it, the less my suspicions made sense. Vivi wasn't the type of person to hurt anyone, even those who deserved it, and during the drive, she'd seemed more like herself, humming along to the radio and trying to get me to open up. She only changed when she was around them.

The headlights of Maria's car penetrated the darkness behind. The vehicle roared as it drove over a thick tree stump.

"This is it." Vivi checked the rearview mirror. "Good, they are here." She cut the engine and stepped out of the car. "I haven't been here since I was a kid."

I blinked, looking around for some indicator that we had arrived, like a sign outside the lodge. Maria's headlight illuminated the thick trunks and leaves dominating the view and making it impossible to see into the distance.

I got out of the passenger seat. Cold settled in my bones. "You do realize we're in the middle of the woods."

"Look." Vivi pointed at a wooden sign nailed into the ground. Brittles Cove. "We can't drive any further."

"What's going on?" Maria stuck her head out of the driver's-side window.

"We're going to take our things and walk from here," Vivi explained, heaving her bags from the trunk. "It's not far."

"I can't walk in these." Tessa angled her leg out of the car from the back seat.

"Then you can stay here." Vivi turned and produced a map from her pocket. Patches of low-trodden grass indicated three paths. "This is the only place you can get good service, so if someone needs to make a call, remember to look for the sign." She pointed at the weathered sign. "If you get lost, head to the cove. There aren't many people around here, but if you're going to be spotted by anyone, it would be there. You should see signs everywhere, but we're going there tomorrow, so I will show you the way." She turned again in the opposite direction, consulting the map.

I didn't know what she was looking for. Every path looked the same.

"I think it's this way. It's the path closest to the sign."

Tessa pushed in front, recording from her cell phone and dragging her suitcase. She trudged a heel out of the ground with each step and offered commentary between ragged breaths.

The rest of us followed. I'd packed light. My backpack was the only thing I had, but I slowed my pace, watching as the girls stopped to catch their breath and clean the dirt blocking the wheels of their suitcases. It took us five minutes to reach the lodge. It looked abandoned. The sloping roof was covered in pine needles, the porch's moss-covered floorboards were splintered, and it was adorned with one worn wooden bench.

The floor creaked as Vivi climbed the steps.

The girls looked over their shoulders and checked their cell phones for service.

Vivi dropped her bags and rattled the key in the lock. The door didn't budge as she pushed.

Harper moaned. "Please don't tell m—"

Vivi threw her shoulder into the door, and it flew back. "Just needed a bit of force," she said as she entered.

We raced in after her, desperate to escape the cold, but the inside wasn't much better. A cruel wind followed us, snaking through the closed doors and windows.

The first room was a living area with worn-out sofas and a TV on the wall above the fireplace. Coffee rings stained the square dinner table separating the small kitchen at the back.

Vivi dropped the map on the table. "I'll show you all to your rooms first, and then we can warm up."

Every room was a replica of the other—two single beds, a chest of drawers filled with a first aid kit, batteries, and a flashlight. Dust coated the window, which had been tied shut.

I dropped my bag on the wooden chair, aware of Vivi's gaze as she pushed her suitcase as far back as it could go under the bed frame.

"Do you want to help me get some wood?" she asked, dropping her handbag on top of the mattress, then she flinched as screams erupted from the room beside us.

"There's a spider," Steph cried.

Vivi blew out a breath, relief etched on her face, but I saw it—unmistakable fear in her eyes.

When she opened the door, the wind picked up, and lights flickered. She trembled as she laughed. "I'll go and deal with the spider, I guess."

I waited alone in the living room, peering out the window into the darkness. Vivi had gone to get logs while the rest of the girls unpacked, put on more makeup, and argued over which beds they were going to sleep in. Small animals chirped and darted through bushes. The wind swept fallen leaves across the ground. My hair stood on end, and I couldn't shake the feeling someone was watching.

"So..." Vivi strolled into the living room, logs in hand. "What do you think of this place?"

I shrugged. "Not what I was expecting."

Vivi nodded. "I know it's not much, but when my family comes here, we want things to be simple. It's a good reminder of the important things in life." She crouched by the fireplace. "I thought it would be best to start a fire now. Tessa keeps threatening to leave if it stays this cold."

I fought the urge to throw water over the embers beginning to light the fireplace and walked to the window overlooking the porch. Then the room went dark, the only source of light the crackling fire. Someone screamed.

Vivi's cell phone lit up. "I forgot to mention that this happens sometimes. It's okay," she shouted. "The lights will come back on soon. Just take one of the flashlights in your drawers."

The floorboard creaked as I felt my way through the narrow hall to the room Vivi and I shared in the farthest part of the lodge.

"I refuse to be cold and stuck in the dark," Tessa screeched.

Vivi's voice carried as she tried to calm her down.

I opened the drawer and pulled out one of the flashlights. The lights flickered, then they were back on.

I inserted batteries into the flashlight and tested it. The bright beam illuminated Vivi's backpack. Something was different. A folded note stuck out from the side. I crossed the room in two paces and took the note.

Two days left. Say your goodbyes.

I turned the paper over. *That's it?*

"What are you doing?"

I jumped, and the paper fluttered to the floor. Vivi leaped forward and snatched it before I could react. Her lips trembled, face ashen.

"What is that?" I asked.

She waved the paper. "Was this you?"

"No, I found it in your bag." My eyes narrowed. "What is happening in two days?"

She pressed her lips together before she exhaled, gaining composure. "I don't know. It's probably just a prank." Her face lightened, but her voice was strained. "You don't have to go through all of my things."

"This isn't the first time?"

"Dani," she said curtly, "for once, please just mind your own business."

She turned her back to me, stuffing the paper into her pocket. Floorboards creaked as she walked away.

I trailed her. The few seconds it took to reach the living area were all she needed to fix her smile in place, but her fingers, tense by her pocket, betrayed her. This trip was going to be more interesting than I'd thought.

"I'm missing Lisa's party to be here." Tessa leaned back into her wooden chair by the kitchen table, her feet hanging off another in front of her.

"However are you going to cope?" I muttered.

Tessa rolled her eyes. "Why are you even here? I thought you hated us."

I pushed her leg off the chair and took a seat. "I do."

"Great, because it's not too late for you to leave."

Harper walked into the room. A loosely fitting brown leather jacket hung off her shoulder.

"For a second, I thought you were Vivi," Tessa said.

I saw it too.

"It's the hoodie," Harper said. "She used to have one like this."

She had that exact one. I recognized the small tear by the neckline from when I borrowed it myself. I looked at Vivi for confirmation, but her eyes rested on the fireplace, worry etched on her face. With Harper, it was more than the hoodie. The hair, the style—everything reminded me of Vivi.

"I wish I had stayed now." Tessa groaned. "Cole was supposed to come see me before we left. He wants to make things official. Lisa heard him telling Stacey."

Harper raised a brow. "Why hasn't he, then?"

"He wants to make it perfect. Flowers, fairy lights, just the two of us. You know? Really romantic."

I laughed. "More romantic than all the times he meets you at parties you're already going to at your best friend's house but barely speaks to you because he is too busy selling drugs?"

Tessa shot up. "Do you think your boyfriend is so much better?"

I smiled as Tessa towered over me. "No. But I don't pretend he is something he isn't."

"Guys." Vivi glared, eyes wide.

"You're jealous." Tessa fell back into her seat, raising her feet onto the table. "Jamie doesn't do anything romantic for you. I was shocked when I heard he wants you to move in with him."

I stilled, the smile on my face slipping.

"Jamie tells Cole things."

I hoped Cole, the ever-romantic, would do us all a favor and push her off a bridge.

She waved the conversation away, raising her voice to be sure Vivi could hear. "I think we should go away once we start Stylies again. Somewhere hot, with a beach, and we can source some of the material ourselves."

"I think it's a good idea." Harper looked over her shoulder. "What about you, Vivi?"

Vivi didn't answer. The TV played quietly in the background, not loudly enough to drown out their voices.

"Vivi?" Harper asked.

She looked up, blinked, and nodded. "I think that would be a good idea."

FIVE

The creak of the floorboards gave her away. Only darkness was visible through the slit in the door, but the sound of slow breathing made me look past that. I leaned forward, squinting, and glared into Maria's narrowed eyes.

I had been searching the room for more notes or something else that could explain Vivi's behavior. Did she know? Was that why she was watching?

I straightened.

Maria pushed the door back, making a show of knocking as it stopped against the wall. "Alone?" She stepped into the room.

"Looks like it."

"That explains why you're searching through Vivi's things." She closed the door behind her, leaning against it until it clicked shut. "I figured we should talk… so you can tell me what you want."

I placed a hand on my chest. "Me? Nothing."

She folded her arms and took in the room, her eyes drawn to the rattle of the window. Maria was the hardest to read. She wasn't like the rest. She didn't have the same interest in Vivi or Stylies, but she always put herself first.

"We need to move on," Maria said. "It's time to let things go."

I smiled. "What exactly are you asking?"

She stepped away from the door. "I don't need to ask, threaten, or beg you for anything. I know you're full of empty threats." She huffed out her chest. It was funny to watch her take my silence for weakness. "You're not going to tell anyone." She uncrossed her arms and straightened. "If you were, you would have done it already. Plus, do you think anyone would believe you?"

I cocked my head. "Are you willing to risk it?"

"It's my word against yours, and everyone knows you're a liar." She reached for the door handle then paused. "This is over."

The wind threw open the door, and then it slammed shut behind her. It had been a while since someone had fought back. It was refreshing. Excitement fluttered in my stomach. Everyone in this house was hiding something, and now seemed like the perfect time to get things off my chest.

My body drew close to Vivi's suitcase tucked under her bed. I trusted no one. Vivi had the right idea bringing a knife. It was just a shame for her that I'd seen her do it. I kneeled by her bed, and dusty floorboards groaned beneath me. I stretched to reach the silver handle of the suitcase. I unzipped it, letting one half fall to the floor before emptying things onto the bed.

I'd watched her pack. I knew the contents—her

perfume, clothes, and a spare handbag. Everything was there. Everything except the knife.

The living room seemed smaller with everyone in it. Steph, Tessa, and I crowded around the coffee table. Harper, Maria, and Vivi took the sofa.

"I never thought I would see the day I missed The Bells." Steph sat beside me and brought a steamy mug to her mouth.

Tessa stood up and scraped her chair across the floorboards, mumbling something about the cold until she placed it by the fireplace and hunched over, shivering.

Harper shrugged, clicking her flashlight on and off as she glanced around the lodge. "I don't mind it. This place is cute." She clicked through channels on the TV, each one responding with static. The howl of the wind picked up, and the screen went blank. "Maybe we should have brought those board games. Don't you have anything here?" Harper turned to Vivi, who shook her head.

I knew someone was watching me. The hairs on my neck stood up, and something tightened in my chest. I looked up, and Maria sank back into the sofa and grinned.

She thought she had called my bluff.

I returned the smile and wet my lips. "You all must be glad Stylies is over."

"It's not over," Tessa snapped. "Jealous? Because we don't want you involved."

I leaned back in my wooden chair, happy someone had

taken the bait. "I wouldn't want to be involved. I can't trust any of you."

They broke into laughter. Steph slammed her mug down on the table. I could admit it was ironic.

Deep lines filled Maria's face as she feigned laughter. She crossed her legs, leaned forward, and soothed the strained muscles on her neck. She should have known better than to taunt me.

"Stylies wouldn't have done any worse with me in it. Your first attempt failed. I won't pretend to know everything about the business. But I do know most of Vivi's hiding places."

The smiles were gone. Their lips parted slightly as they sat up, but I was only interested in Maria. Intense satisfaction radiated through me as she clenched her fists by her side.

This was the beauty of a secret. As long as it was something the owner didn't want known, it had power. *I* had power.

The pleasure of watching Maria squirm was fading. I'd sat on this for too long, and now she believed I was all talk, no action. I needed to remind her and everyone else why I was a threat.

I crossed my arms. "Didn't you ever wonder how you lost so much so quickly?"

Maria's eyes flashed.

"Vivi noticed," I continued. "Why do you think she doesn't want to go back into business with you?"

"I know what you're suggesting, and none of us would do that." Tessa waved a hand. "Not everyone is like you.

Selfish, takes what they want without caring who they hurt."

"Really?" I raised a brow. I could practically see beads of sweat on Maria's forehead.

They wouldn't believe me, but all they had to do was look at Vivi. She folded herself into a ball, her arms wrapped around her legs. All eyes traveled to hers. Only I felt the weight of Maria's. They were planted on me and filled with rage.

"Vivi?" Steph prompted. "Is it true?"

Vivi shrugged. "I don't know."

Harper turned and pulled Vivi's arms out from under her. "What do you mean you don't know?"

"The numbers were weird. It didn't add up. I thought someone might have taken the money." Vivi looked up at me, hard-eyed. "I couldn't be sure."

"But it's possible?" Tessa asked.

Vivi nodded, wrapping her arms around herself.

Steph jerked her head in my direction. "Or she could be lying. It wouldn't be the first time."

"Who?" Harper glared at me. "You wouldn't bring it up if you didn't know who it was."

I pursed my lips.

Harper crossed the room. "I know you're taking pleasure in all of this."

Maria cleared her throat. "Just ignore her. She loves the attention. She wants to create a divide between us."

Harper ignored her. "Who was it?"

All eyes were on me, and my grin was almost uncontrollable. I was pleased with my decision to come to the lodge.

"Maria." The name felt sweet on my lips.

The room fell silent.

Maria's jaw dropped.

Something in my chest fluttered at the shocked expressions.

I'd expected her to deny it or to lash out in a rage. Either would have been enjoyable. But she was smart. She was trapped miles away from home with the friends she had stolen over twenty grand from. An explanation wouldn't be enough.

Maria's head fell into her hands. "I'm so sorry. It's been eating me up."

"What has?" Harper pushed Maria's hands away from her face.

She looked up, tears brimming her small eyes. "I took the money."

Vivi shook her head.

Steph shot up. Chair legs scraped across the floor. "After everything we put into this?"

They surrounded Maria. Vivi watched on from the edge of the sofa.

Maria wasn't relaxed now. Her shoulders were hunched, and her hands gripped her hair. "I wanted to tell you guys, but I panicked. I got laid off. I planned to pay it back, but I just couldn't get back on track."

"Laid off?" Harper's index finger and thumb clutched Maria's chin. "And you thought it would be a good idea to steal from us?"

Maria grimaced. "No, of course not. You're my friends. I would never want to hurt you."

Liar.

Maria knotted her hands together. "I'm sorry."

She isn't.

Vivi watched the exchange, lips pressed tightly, eyes wide as she hugged herself. She didn't need the money. She was probably happy to have an excuse not to work with them. She couldn't trust them, and someone was threatening her. Maria? Maybe Maria felt guilty for taking the money and wanted to pressure Vivi into restarting the business. I wondered if Vivi was thinking the same thing.

"I want it back," Harper hissed.

Maria held out her hands. "How am I going to get that kind of money?"

Harper leaned in, spit flying. "I don't care if you have to steal it from someone else."

It lasted only a second. But the mask slipped. Maria bared her teeth, flaring her nostrils. But she rearranged her face as Harper threw her arm back and swung. Tessa and Steph dived forward, pulling Harper back before she could connect.

"Get off me." She pushed them off.

Maria wiped at her cheek, but not a single tear fell from her eyes.

The room quieted as Vivi stood. Maria had taken the most from Vivi. Vivi had the most reason to be angry.

Vivi loomed over Maria, her face unreadable, then Vivi opened her arms and embraced Maria. "You should have come to us if you needed it. We would have supported you."

I blinked. Even Maria couldn't hide the surprise on her face.

Could Vivi not see it? Was she too blind or too stupid? Or maybe it just took a liar to spot one.

SIX

Tension weighed heavy in the air as Vivi held Maria close, muttering reassurances over the crackling of the fire. The static hum of the TV provided an awkward backdrop. The other girls glared. Their main objective was to get Vivi to agree to start Stylies again. It worked in their favor if she forgave Maria. They exchanged knowing looks, as though they knew they had no option but to play along.

Harper slammed a hand against the back of the TV, and a metal clang rang around the room. The screen cleared, and an audible voice gave the latest news report.

Vivi clapped her hands together. "We should lighten the mood a little." She pulled out a small gift wrapped in silver. "Let's start with presents."

"Maria," Harper called, "considering you stole from us, I'm going to keep your gift."

Maria released a tense laugh.

I leaned back into the kitchen cabinet as they huddled around the sofa and passed gifts around the room. They were beaming and hugging as they unwrapped the paper.

Vivi joined me in the kitchen. "I'm sure if the others knew you were coming, they would have gotten you something." She passed a wrapped box into my hands.

I rubbed my chin. "There's been a mistake."

Vivi shook her head. "No, it's yours."

Something tightened in my throat. I shook the box. A light clatter sounded from inside. "Are they your keys to The Bells because you're leaving?"

She smiled. "Nothing that good."

I opened the box. A silver bracelet lay at the bottom. I cleared the thickness in my throat, now acutely aware we had an audience of beady eyes trying to determine its worth.

I took out the bracelet, heat rising at the back of my eyes. "Thanks."

Vivi leaned in. "I'd be happy to exchange it."

I shut the lid. "I don't have anything to exchange it for."

Vivi held my gaze, her jaw tense.

"How about you? Are you ready to talk about the gift someone left in your room?"

She inhaled and stepped back. "Drop it."

"Sorry, Dani, no gift," Steph groaned. "I didn't know you were coming, but even if I did—"

Vivi nudged her as she passed. "Be nice."

"No way," Harper exclaimed, clutching on to tickets, then screeched, "You didn't!" She threw her arms around Vivi's neck. "I have been trying to see Wynn live in theatre for ages."

Vivi shrugged. "My mom knows one of the actors."

I held the box, given in pity, in hope for the return of something I hadn't stolen. It could be nice to have friends, people who cared, but that was not what these girls were. I saw through the fake smiles as they thanked each other, crushing wrapping paper into balls and throwing them into the fire.

I opened the cabinets and pulled out the drawers. There was only one large pot, three mugs, a rusted teaspoon, a bent fork, and a dull knife.

"There is no cutlery here," Vivi called over her shoulder. She held up a bag. "We normally bring our own. I've got some wooden ones here."

"Thank you," I managed through gritted teeth, more interested in the missing knife she'd brought. I bent over to close the drawer then stopped.

I felt her before I saw her. Something jolted in my neck.

"Nice try." Maria sneered. She leaned forward, her back to the living room. "It's pathetic. That was all you had. If anything, it's brought us closer together."

"Is that what you think?"

Maria's eyes flashed.

I stepped out of the kitchen. "Let's play a game. Truth or dare."

"I dare you to go home," Steph cried.

The girls laughed.

Harper rubbed at her wrist. "That seems like the worst possible game to play with you."

"Let's play," Vivi said, her eyes fixed on mine. "I'll start. Dani, truth or dare?"

I smiled. "Truth."

"I already know you stole my bracelet. I want to know what you did with it."

I wet my lips, and Harper shuffled in her seat.

My revelation with Maria hadn't gone according to plan, so I thought I would keep this one to myself. "You can have this back." I threw the box in her direction. "I didn't take your bracelet."

She sighed. "It got up and left The Bells by itself?"

"No," I said slowly. "I don't think it left The Bells."

"If you know something, just say it." Steph rolled her eyes.

I pursed my lips.

"Nothing? Great. What a waste of time," Steph said.

"I'll go," I said. "Steph, how many people have agreed to vote for you just to get me off the swim team?"

She flashed her teeth. "You're supposed to ask, 'Truth or dare?' But I'll answer your question because there isn't anything you can do about it." She tapped her right index finger along the fingers on her left hand, humming to herself. "Two. The others are voting for me because they think I'll be a good leader."

I gritted my teeth. I only knew about one.

Steph turned to Maria. "Maria, truth or dare?"

Maria tilted her head to the ceiling. "Dare."

"I dare you to swap beds with me."

"No," Maria called. "I'm not going anywhere near the side with the spider."

Steph raised her palms. "So are you forfeiting?"

Maria swallowed. "No. Fine." She looked around the room. "Harper, I dare you to choose one of our bags to hide outside. Whoever it is has to find it later."

"Wait," Steph called. "It not your tur—"

Harper didn't waste a second. She grabbed Maria's bag before she could pull it out of the way.

"Wait!" Maria cried. "You weren't supposed to choose me."

Harper was already out the door. A harsh breeze lashed through the lodge. We rushed to the window and perched on the windowsill, watching through the circles of water as Harper blended with the darkness.

She came back ten minutes later.

"Really?" Maria frowned. "Why would you choose me?"

Harper ignored her. Shivering, she rushed into her room and returned with a duvet over her shoulders. "I have a question for Vivi." She scratched the bottom of her chin. "And I want you to think carefully before you answer."

Silence fell in the room.

"Why did you want us all here?" Harper asked.

Vivi's brow furrowed. "What do you mean? You're all my friends." She glanced at me but didn't amend her statement. "I wanted to spend time with you away from campus."

"Your friends?" Harper echoed.

Something unspoken hung in the air. The girls sensed it too.

Vivi tensed. "Of course. Why would you even question that?"

Harper pulled back her duvet and dropped a cloth on the table. Something glinted inside. I recognized it. So did Vivi. Her eyes flashed white.

Veins protruded from Harper's knuckles. "So why the knife?"

A buzzing rang in my head. How had Harper gotten to the knife before I could?

"Harper, what's going on?" Tessa shot up, heels clicking against the wooden floor. "This isn't funny."

Vivi glared at it, eyes glazed, lips pinned between her teeth.

Harper ignored Tessa. She was waiting for an answer from Vivi.

"Why were you going through her things?" I asked.

Harper cocked her head. "The person you're sharing a room with brings a knife, and you're asking why I was looking?"

The knife wasn't the issue for me. It was who had it.

"Vivi?" Tessa tugged on her shoulder. "Is it true?"

Vivi didn't move. She sniffed. Tears laced her lashes. "I'm sorry." Her voice cracked.

No one moved to comfort her.

"Obviously, I wouldn't use it on any of you. I've had it with me for a few weeks. I just needed to feel safe."

Tessa gasped. "From us?"

"I don't know who," Vivi murmured, running a hand over her forehead. "Someone has been threatening me."

I watched their reactions. Someone was faking it. Brows furrowed with concern. Mouths opened with shock.

"Leaving handwritten notes with my things," Vivi continued. "I found the first one in class, and the first thing I wanted to do was tell you guys." Vivi wiped at her cheek. "Then I started getting them in The Bells, in my room."

Steph's head snapped in my direction, and it wasn't long before the rest followed.

I rolled my eyes. "I would simply threaten her to her face."

"It's not Dani." Vivi shook her head. "I have gotten the

notes when she wasn't around. I thought it could be one of you. It's the only thing that started to make any sense."

Maria stepped forward, placing a hand on her lap. "Come on. None of us would do that."

I hummed. "Just like you wouldn't steal?"

Maria scowled, wetting her lips. "What do the notes say?"

Vivi swallowed. "I am going to die."

Silence. Eyes swept the room.

"Each note has a number counting down, and I don't have any time left." Vivi clasped a hand around her mouth and sobbed.

Steph pulled out her cell phone. "We should call the police."

Vivi shook her head. "They aren't going to do anything. Nothing has actually happened. They'll see it as a prank and think I'm paranoid."

"Has anything else weird been happening?" Maria asked.

Vivi nodded. "I've had things go missing, people claiming to know me who I've never met."

"Like the guy from this morning," Harper said through a breath. "It's happened before?"

"It's like someone else is pretending to be me." Vivi reached into her pocket and pulled out the note. "This was the latest one."

The girls huddled around her. Harper held the knife between her thighs.

The concern looked genuine. It would be. They couldn't restart Stylies if Vivi was dead.

Steph scrubbed her face. "But why would you bring us all to the lodge if someone was threatening to kill you?"

I willed her to keep quiet. She couldn't trust them.

"I have a few days left, and I wanted to believe it wasn't one of you." Vivi's hand squeezed on the paper. "But Dani found this one in my room in the lodge."

None of the girls said anything. Eyes roamed the semi-circle around Vivi they had created.

"This sounds like Dani's idea of a joke," Steph said. "Or something someone would do to get back at her, not you."

I inhaled. "The note was on her bag."

Harper didn't glance up. "Could someone have put it there before you left?"

My stomach clenched. It would be impossible. It was on top of her bag, not in it.

Vivi's brows furrowed. "I don't kn—maybe."

I bit my tongue.

"I was in a rush, so maybe I didn't check my bag properly."

Tessa stroked Vivi's hair. "I think you're really worried and starting to overthink things."

Steph agreed. "We can report this when we get back."

Maria took her hand. "You're here with all of us. Nothing is going to happen to you."

Harper nodded, meeting my eyes—and never letting go of the knife.

SEVEN

Vivi had been at The Bells two days before I moved in. She greeted me with fancy chocolate, a gift bath set, and a genuine smile, unlike the ones she forced lately. After a few days, I realized I would never have friends at The Bells. It didn't bother me, but it mattered to Vivi. That was her first mistake.

She got the friends she wanted, and even now, she leaned on them as they huddled around her, despite knowing there was a good chance one of them wanted her dead. She couldn't trust them, but she had already let them in, and they wouldn't stop until they got what they wanted.

"I think I need to get some fresh air." Vivi stood up, pulling away from their embrace.

"Let's all go," Harper suggested, already zipping her jacket around her, the knife nowhere in sight.

Unease gripped my stomach.

"Yeah." Vivi's face darkened. "That's a good idea."

They leaped up.

"Wait," Tessa said. "I've got the perfect outfit for th—"

The girls groaned.

"Are you going to explain to my social media followers why I'm wearing these boots with this shirt?" Tessa gripped the hem of her top. Black sequins offered a muted shine. "Especially if we're starting Stylies again."

We stood on the front porch of the lodge. No one committed to moving any farther than the entrance. The wooden bench creaked every time Tessa adopted a new pose for a photo. The fire still burned in the lodge. The soft glow of light was taunting as cold settled into our skin.

Harper picked up a stick, destroying a spiderweb before she threw it into the distance.

"I think I'll call my parents," Vivi said. "I should have let them know when we got here."

Steph hooked her arm around Vivi's. "I'll come with you."

Vivi shook her head and shuffled from her grip. "I'll be quick. I made the mistake of telling them about the notes, so they worry if they don't hear from me. You guys should look around and get familiar with Brittles Cove."

"Do you think it's a good idea for you to be alone right now?" Tessa asked.

Vivi rubbed her hands along her thigh. "I'll be fine."

Harper opened her mouth then closed it.

How did we know she wasn't getting into her car and leaving right now? Hairs rose at the back of my neck. She wasn't going to leave me alone with them.

"Wait," Harper called. "Where are your car keys?"

Vivi's eyes narrowed. "In the lodge."

"Good," Harper said.

Vivi walked away, her flashlight bobbing ahead of her.

"I better go and start searching for my bag," Maria said. "Thanks for that, Harper. I couldn't even see where you went through the window. At least give me a clue."

"No." Harper shook her head. "Consider this the start of the payback for stealing from us."

Tessa rose from the bench. "You almost put Vivi off working with any of us again."

"She still hasn't agreed to anything," Maria said, leading the way down the steps.

"She will." Harper followed behind.

I hung over the wooden beam as they walked away, like they had forgotten I was there. I gazed up. The stars were clear in the sky, the moon shining over their silhouettes as they faded into the trees, their plans to use Vivi taken by the wind.

I waited until I was sure no one was coming back before I entered the lodge. I started with Harper and Tessa's room. The smell of damp soil filled the air. I didn't know what I was looking for, but I wasn't stupid enough to trust anyone here. Moonlight filtered through the window, highlighting the unnatural bump in Harper's bedding. I pulled back the tightly tucked duvet. Her backpack lay in the center.

I opened it. The brown wrapping Candice had given to Harper was inside. It was light. As I opened it, the rustle seemed to amplify. The thin walls allowed the sound to escape, as though calling the girls back. I took out the ID card inside, and my heart stilled.

Harper looked back at me. She had a middle part in her

light-brown hair, extensions lengthening her blunt bob. She looked different. She looked li—

I swallowed the lump in my throat as I read the name printed beside the picture. Vivienne Demi Marks.

Something clicked. This wasn't the first time Harper had impersonated Vivi. Her desperation to get Luke away from Vivi wasn't about her trying to protect a friend but herself.

Candice laughed at the rumors that she sold fake IDs, but she'd never denied them. I wouldn't have to convince Vivi that Harper had stolen her bracelet when I could show her this.

I pushed the ID into my pocket and placed the bag back where I'd found it, tucking in the sheets at the corners. I moved to Tessa's bags, which were already open on the chair. Glittery clothes were strewn about. Everyone else had knitted sweaters, and Tessa had two sparkly off-the-shoulder dresses in red and black so she could match them according to the sunset. I riffled past a sparkly bikini to the rest of the contents, finding nothing interesting or practical.

In Maria and Steph's room, Maria's suitcase was filled with clothes. I moved to Steph's, and after I was satisfied there was nothing to find but clothes and makeup, I poured the bag out for my amusement.

Darkness cloaked my room at the back of the lodge. The little heat from the living room didn't penetrate these walls. Shivering, I emptied Vivi's bag. I already knew what was inside. This time, I needed something else—her car key.

I thought I knew my housemates and their secrets, but I had underestimated what they were capable of. Scrunched-up papers lay at the bottom—the notes, each one counting down. A number and a threat.

Five days. Enjoy every breath.

Four days. You'll be missed.

Three days. Enjoy your trip.

I pushed the notes back inside, pressed the cool metal of Vivi's car key into my palm, slipped it into my pocket, then left.

I swung my flashlight, and cold wind whipped around my face and hair, drowning out the faint crunch of leaves. I squinted, trying to locate the sound of voices. The girls had gone farther than I thought. I didn't move too far from the lodge. I could still see it through the mass of trees behind me.

I jumped, turning just as Steph stepped out. Alone. She shielded her eyes as I pointed the light at her before lowering it to the ground. "Where's everyone else?"

Steph tutted. "You know no one wants you here, and Vivi just feels sorry for you."

"You don't want me here because you're bitter I beat you in practice three times a week."

Her jaw ticked. "You won't be on the team for much longer."

Excitement bubbled in my stomach. "It's funny you say that, because Coach wants to speak with you. I got the feeling you would be dropped from the team."

Steph's throat worked.

"After today's practice, I spoke to Coach about how you tried to convince others to vote for you because you would guarantee I wouldn't be on the team next year, and she agreed it wouldn't be appropriate to have someone on the team, let alone captaining, with that kind of attitude. Of course, she thought it would be best coming from her. She wanted to have a quiet word with you when we got back. But I don't know." I shrugged. My lips spread in a wide smile. "I guess I just couldn't keep the good news to myself."

She lunged too quickly for me to react. Her fist collided with my stomach. Sharp pain radiated beneath my ribs. I staggered back, her fist grazing my cheek. I shielded my face, my arms raised as Steph continued her erratic blows. Buzzing issued from my head. And it took a moment for me to realize she was speaking.

"No one cares about you." She grunted, delivering each word with a blow.

I fell to the ground—cold stone and dirt embedding in my nails as I tried to push up, catching the words, alone and desperate. I sat back and observed, identifying ways to exploit people's weaknesses and being aware of my own. I couldn't fight.

I managed to get onto my back, kicking air as Steph moved back. I regained my breath, my body relaxing as shimmering boots blocked Steph from view.

"She's not worth it." Tessa stepped between us. "She will get what's coming to her." She didn't glance back as she patted Steph on the shoulder.

Steph hunched over, her hands on her knees as she breathed deeply. "I know."

"Remember, we're here to convince Vivi, and this isn't going to help."

That got through to Steph. She straightened, rubbing at her hands. It always came back to Vivi.

I stayed on the floor, clutching my stomach. Something twitched and ached, but I couldn't help but smile.

Steph watched. The satisfaction on her face turned to confusion. "I don't know how you can keep smiling after that pathetic attempt at a fight."

I remembered what Coach had said. Unless Steph was a physical threat, there was nothing she could do to have her removed from the team. "If you weren't going to be kicked off the team before, you definitely are now."

Anger flared in her narrowed eyes. There was a zero-tolerance policy for violence, and Steph knew it.

I winced as laughter rumbled in my stomach.

Steph pulled her lips back against her teeth. The metal of her braces flashed as she drew her legs back. I readied myself for another blow.

"Come on." Tessa held her back.

They turned, and I pressed my head against the damp soil, hearing rather than seeing their retreat. It was hard to breathe. The pain in my stomach pulsed. I leaned against a tree, readying to propel myself up. Then I saw a flash. I blinked, unsure if the pain had somehow affected my vision. Then I saw it again—a small beam of light appeared out of nowhere. Then I made out the bright red of Vivi's jacket. I sank low, my head inches from the ground. Anyone else would see me and laugh. I could handle that. What I didn't want was Vivi's pity.

She moved slowly through the trees, holding her cell phone as the flashlight function barely shone in the black. I held my breath as she moved farther into the shadows, as though any movement would give my position away.

A figure all in black followed Vivi, hood up. I leaned forward. We were the only ones here. Steph and Tessa had left in the opposite direction. It could only be Maria or Harper, but only one person was unmistakably identifiable by their height. Harper.

She moved through the trees, neck craning as she followed the small beam of light Vivi provided. Pieces slotted into place. The notes left for Vivi had come from The Bells, from someone who had taken their obsession with Vivi to the extreme and now wanted her life. Harper had stolen Vivi's bracelet, created a fake ID, and taken the knife. Now she was following Vivi.

My heart clattered. I wouldn't be quick enough to catch up without being noticed, but I had to get closer. I propped myself up on my elbows, grunting. I rose to my feet, a fore-boding feeling creeping down my spine, blood pumping faster. Perhaps on any other day, I would have listened to the warning signs, but I bit my lip, suppressing the pain, and followed.

EIGHT

I fought the urge to call out as I trailed farther into the woods, too slow to keep up with Harper and Vivi and too far gone to turn back. One arm hugged my body, and my toes were numb in my boots. An unnerving feeling clawed in my stomach. I couldn't be sure I wasn't going in circles, surrounded by nothing but thick trees. I relied on the moonlight filtering through to avoid stepping on any branches or leaves that would give me away. My head was laced with sweat, and my hand instinctively reached for my cell phone before I remembered it was useless.

I still had the key. I could go back to the car—the only place to get a signal, according to Vivi. I just had to look for the Brittles Cove sign. *But where was it?* I turned. Something caught my feet, and I stumbled, breath hitching. My stomach lurched, and my arm reached out, barely managing to hold my weight as I fell against a tree trunk.

That was when I heard the voices. Distorted by the wind at first, they became clearer as I moved closer, each step deliberate and softened by patches of soil. I held my breath. I couldn't see the owners of the voices, but I was close.

"I don't get it. We are friends." Vivi's voice was unmistakable, but her tone was different. A note of fear registered.

"Were we?" Harper hissed. "Because it never felt equal. Everything is always about you—boys, business, friends. No one acknowledged me until I was around you. Became you."

I shuffled around a tree, edging my head out until they came into view.

Harper faced Vivi, with her back to me.

Vivi frowned. "I don't understand."

"Of course you wouldn't, because I was always happy enough to take your scraps." Harper's arm jerked. "All my so-called friends only looked at me once you acknowledged my existence. We would go out, and boys never spoke to me. If they did, it was because I was standing next to you. How could I compete?" She shook her head. "I couldn't. But then I pretended to be you and got everything I wanted. How does it feel? To know you're holding the lives of your friends in your hands?" Harper's head tilted, the wind catching her hair.

It wasn't a rhetorical question, and Vivi had no answer. I remembered the moment everything had changed. Stylies was meant to be a fun project. Then they started dreaming big—international shipping, an office, and a billboard Tessa had made so she could add modeling to her resume. Their spending had continued to increase, and only Vivi had contributed more. By the time she'd realized, it was too late.

Vivi ran her hands through her hair. "All I wanted was to help."

"Yeah? But we all know Mabel's scholarship has been canceled. She can barely make it through to next year as it is. Steph has had to miss swim meets to work because you stopped Stylies, but you don't want to give the business another go?" Harper jabbed a finger at her. "No. Because you like knowing we are at your mercy."

Vivi's lips pressed into a thin line. "You know it's not like that. I lost a lot too. I don't want to put my parents through that again."

"Really?" Harper scoffed. "You lost a lo—" She broke into a laugh as her hair whipped around her. "It doesn't matter anyway. I don't need you anymore. I can have everything I want without you."

My stomach closed in on itself as I crept forward.

Harper's neck flexed. "I thought you had realized it was me. That's why you invited me here, why you brought the knife."

Vivi shook her head. "What are you talking about?"

"The notes."

"I was right." Vivi clutched her chest, shuddering as she drew in air. "All of you?"

"No, just me." Harper smiled. "I have to admit it was fun watching you squirm. Every time you found a note, you became more willing to help us. You even stopped shutting down Tessa's stupid ideas. But now I know there are faster ways to get what I want. What *we* want. I'm just willing to go a little further to get it. It worked, didn't it? The only reason you were even considering starting Stylies again was because of the threats. Not because you care about any of us." She raised her palms. "I know you too well, Vivi. I've learned how to play the part. With strangers, friends, family."

Vivi stepped back, eyes bulging, and a shaky hand covered her lips.

"Luke was so angry with me when I tried to keep him away from you," Harper snarled. "He didn't realize it was me he was in love with. Do you know how hard it was to watch him cry over you?"

"I don't." Vivi cupped her face. "I didn—"

"You don't deserve any of it!" Harper screamed. The shrill sound echoed through the trees, then everything went still.

My muscles tensed. Adrenaline raced through my body.

"What's going on here?" Maria emerged from the shadows. Clothes overflowed from her backpack and hung over her shoulder and dirt-stained arms.

"Maria." Vivi sounded breathless. She shuffled closer to her. "Talk to her. Sh—"

"I planned to." Maria threw down her bag. "The dare was to hide the bag, not scatter my things all over the woods." She paused. Her words met silence. She drew her head back, eyes darting from Vivi to Harper. "What have I missed?"

"Please," Vivi said. "Talk to her. She thinks I am trying to control you guys."

There was a pause. Time seemed to slow as Maria looked between them. Something shifted, and Maria shrugged. "Aren't you?"

Vivi slowly shook her head, her mouth opening and closing. Then she took steps back. Watching the realization of betrayal on her face was a weird feeling. Only moments ago, she had comforted Maria, forgiving her for stealing. She wanted to move past it and believe it was a lapse in judgment and not a demonstration of her character, but all she did was give Maria another opportunity to stab her in the back.

Vivi swallowed. "I care about all of you. But sometimes I feel like I can't trust you. Why would I want to be in business with you?"

"Guys?"

Voices called from behind the trees, flashlights bobbed, twigs cracked under boots. Steph and Tessa approached.

"Oh, good, we're all here," Tessa said.

"Where's Dani?" Maria asked.

I pressed my back against the tree, held my breath, and squeezed my eyes shut. A persistent thud echoed through my body. I waited for someone to call out. No one did.

"I might have accidentally lost it with her. So she's probably back at the lodge trying to steal all our things," Steph said.

I let out a breath, creeping forward as an uncomfortable silence fell.

"What's going on here?" Steph's eyes narrowed.

Vivi pinched at her temples, her loose hair ruffled by the wind. "Harper was just telling me how she thinks I'm a bad friend." There was a question in there. Her eyes gleamed with hope, pleading for at least one of them to be on her side.

Tessa scowled. "Selfish seems more accurate."

Vivi shook her head. "You too?" She took a step back.

The girls closed in around her.

"I don't think there's been a day where you haven't

tried to use me for something," Vivi said. The thickness in her voice increased, but there was something else—a newfound determination. "I tried to move past it, tell myself that friends helped each other. But no friend would send threatening notes and watch as I fell apart."

Tessa stepped forward. "Vivi, we told you. It wa—"

"It was her." Vivi's cry rang out. She jabbed a finger in Harper's direction.

"Stop being dramatic." Harper held out her palms. "You're here, aren't you? It was the only way I could help you make better decisions."

"Harper," Tessa called. "You didn't have to go so far."

"You still need Stylies, don't you?" Harper's lip curled. "She would have left, and we would have had nothing. Well, we would have been fine if someone hadn't been stealing from her the whole time."

Maria opened her mouth to speak, but Harper cut her off. "Don't worry. I don't completely blame you. There's only so much we can do when we're working with a narcissist."

"Because I don't want to go into business with you?" Vivi asked. "Maria admitted to stealing. You have been impersonating me and threatening to kill me, and Tessa is more interested in trying to become famous than the brand. Is it really any surprise that I don't want to waste money on you? I have tried with all of you. I kept telling myself it would get better because you're all my friends, but with friends like you, who needs enemies?"

"Vivi, you're being ridiculous." Steph moved toward her, resting her palm on Vivi's shoulder.

Vivi shrugged her off. "I don't need any of you. You

need me." She tapped her fist to her chest. "And I don't know why it has taken this long for me to see it. I could leave The Bells tomorrow, and nothing in my life would change."

Vivi stepped back, brushing past Steph. "You know, I think I will leave. You guys can figure out how to suck the life out of someone else, and I'm sure the police would be interested in hearing about some of the things you guys have been up to. You know it's illegal to pretend to be someone else, right? The money taken from the business. The accounts opened in my name. It's all making sense."

"We won't let you." Harper lunged forward. She was quick, too quick for Vivi to react. Something glinted in the light as she moved. It wasn't until she was in front of Vivi that I saw the knife.

NINE

I shuddered. My hand slipped, scraping against the rough tree bark. Blood trickled from my palm, but I kept my eyes on Harper. Pain rippled through my stomach, urging me to sink farther into the shadows. I resisted.

"Harper, no," Tessa cried. The high-pitched scream pierced the cold air.

Harper waved the knife teasingly.

Palms raised, Vivi shuffled back. The silent retreat was her only response.

"Harper?" Steph called, but she didn't move. None of them did.

Harper closed in on Vivi, her grip tightening on the knife. Veins protruded from her pale knuckles.

Vivi chanced a wary glance over her shoulder. She looked back at the girls. Her friends seemed to be weighing their options. "You're not going to stab me." She stopped and straightened. "Think about it. You'll go to prison for the rest of your life. Would it be worth it? In front of three witnesses with everything else you've done?"

Harper slowed her movements then pressed the knife against Vivi's cheek.

Vivi tensed but continued. "It probably won't take long for them to find the trail you've left behind. All the times you've pretended to be me."

I thought about the fake ID in my pocket. Harper would never be happy living in Vivi's shadow. She didn't just want everything she had. She wanted to become her.

"Come on, Harper. Don't do anything stupid," Steph called.

Harper pulled back the knife. Her hold loosened. She glared as though it were unfamiliar, taking half a step back and blinking slowly. Then she slashed.

A line of crimson broke the surface of Vivi's cheek. She recoiled, her hands flying to her face.

"Happy now?" Harper adjusted her body for another attack.

Tessa and Steph were on her, pulling her back.

Maria smirked as she watched.

"What are you doing?" Steph shoved Harper then froze, her eyes wide. "Look." Steph clasped her hands together. "We're friends. We need to sit down and speak about all of this."

It was too late. Vivi had seen her opportunity. Her whole body tensed, and her hair flailed behind her as she ran.

I held my breath, willing her to move faster. The wind tugged at her clothes as she sliced through the air, not sparing a glance backward.

That was how she missed Maria crashing into step beside her and why she couldn't evade the leg swung into her path. Vivi smacked into the ground. Maria leaned over her, grabbing her by the arm and pulling her up to drag her back to Harper.

"Stop," Tessa screeched. She turned to Harper. "What if she goes to the police? She's already going to leave The Bells the first chance she gets. I can't be involved in any of this. Everything I have is tied up in this business."

Harper jutted her chin. "Because it will ruin your chances of becoming famous?"

Tessa chewed her lip.

"It's barely a cut." Harper flexed her neck. "She'll live. If you want to blame someone for Vivi leaving, it's Maria."

Maria gulped.

"It was never for Vivi to forgive," Harper said. "She has so much money that she didn't even notice anything was missing. No, it's us you really stole from."

Maria stepped back, leaving Vivi crumpled on the floor. "I still have it. I didn't spend it. I can give it all back. And I'll talk to Vivi. We can fix this, and we can all work together again."

Harper dropped her arm. "She will never forgive me for what I've done."

Vivi exhaled, clutching her thigh.

Harper rubbed her neck. "So what should we do with her?"

Tessa's eyes widened. "What do you mean?"

"You said it yourself." Harper shrugged. "She's going to leave The Bells, and we can't risk her going to the police."

My heart rattled in my chest. Hidden in the cloak of darkness, I didn't move. Vivi's car keys burned a hole in my pocket. I wasn't much safer here than Vivi. I gritted my teeth, pushing off the tree. I needed to call for help, but if Vivi managed to get away, she wouldn't stay here. What would she do next? Go to the cove, where there was a better chance of being discovered, or to the car to call for help? I decided to worry about that later. I silently clawed back leaves and branches then headed back to the cars.

My heart clattered in my chest. I almost collapsed in relief at the sight of Vivi's black Audi. No one else was here. I stumbled forward, unlocking the car. A short click broke the stillness. Headlights flashed. I waited to be sure no one else heard, then I saw it. I fell to my knees, relief short-lived. My nails clung to the damp earth.

"No," I breathed, squeezing my eyes shut.

Someone had cut the tires. Only Vivi's tires. I clamped down on my lips and balled my hands into fists. Maria's car was still here, untouched.

I got into the driver's seat. Two bars of service were visible in the corner of my cell phone. My fingers were numb as I made the first call.

Jamie picked up on the third ring.

"Jamie, I'll explain everything when you get here, but you need to come to Brittles Cove right now."

Panic crept into his voice. "What's going on?"

"I don't have time right now. Just promise me you'll come?"

"Dani? You're worrying me."

"I have to go."

"Wait, stay on the c—"

I hung up. My fingers were trembling as I made the next call.

I didn't know how much of it was an act. My voice shook, tears pooled, and I struggled to breathe as I relayed everything that had happened to the emergency operator. When the police came, they were going to see me as much as a victim as Vivi. I hugged my body. I didn't want to go back there. I tapped my feet. Every breath of the frigid, icy air was harder to take than the last. I stared through the car's layer of frost. Shadows moved outside. Hope rose in my chest. Maybe it was Vivi. Maybe she was safe and we just had to wait in the car until Jamie or the police arrived. But shadows continued to fall, and no one came.

It should have been easy. I'd spent the whole year ignoring everything they had done to Vivi, but her life had never been at risk. I shook my head, at odds with my own decision. She was outnumbered, and she had no chance against Harper. I groaned into my palms. I left the car, dragging my body forward before I could give myself time to change my mind.

They were gone.

My breaths evened out as I edged out of the trees. The open air was heavy, and away from the blanket of leaves, I felt eyes on me. I moved quickly along the thinning earth. Small pools of blood were the only proof they had ever been there. I kept moving. There was little space to hide. Trees became sparse. Damp soil turned to thick rock. Moonlight reached the floor's surface, wind whistling over faint laps of water, salt heavy in the air. I had found Brittles Cove —and Vivi. Her jacket was crimson in the light. She hunched over on the ground, holding her left thigh.

I buried myself under the thin canopy of the leaves. The cops were coming. I just needed Vivi to make it until they arrived. I'd done all I could without putting myself at risk.

The jagged edge of the cove lay bare, exposing four figures in the center. Tessa and Steph hung back. Their arms were wrapped around their bodies as they watched Maria and Harper tower over Vivi.

"I want to help you, Vivi," Maria hissed.

Vivi winced and kicked out, her strike catching the air.

Maria laughed and stepped within reach of Vivi's foot. "This is your last chance."

Vivi hesitated. Glassy eyes glared. She tried again, thrusting out her leg, then screamed in pain as Maria swatted it away.

Harper cupped her hands to her mouth. "Dani!" she cried.

I stilled. *Why is she calling me?*

Maria nudged her.

"We need to do something about her, or she will sell us out as soon as we get back." Harper turned and called again.

Using her hands and one leg, Vivi shuffled back. She bit down on her lip, and blood from the slash rolled down her cheek. She looked over the coastline; slaps of the waves intensified.

I couldn't see over the edge, but Vivi could. She hobbled up on one leg and squeezed her eyes shut.

Tessa swallowed. "We have to call an ambulance."

Harper's head snapped back. "What do you think will happen to us if we do that?"

"Us?" Steph scoffed.

Harper's hand tensed. There was only one person to blame. Unfortunately for them, it was the person holding the knife.

Tessa's eyes bulged. "I know we're angry and have every right to be. But she's still our friend."

Harper cackled, wild and mechanical. "She's planning to leave as soon as we get back. Do you really want to be the face of a failed business?"

Tessa flinched.

"How much is it you owe her, Maria? Twenty grand? You can wipe that debt right here. Tessa, Stylies was your idea, but she doesn't want you to be the face of it. She thinks you make it look cheap. If you guys want something, take it." Harper raised the knife to point at Steph. "You want Dani off the swim team?"

The girls blinked and exchanged unsure glances. Maria, though, grinned.

"Tessa," Vivi pleaded. "Please."

They drew their heads back, as though they had forgotten she was there.

Vivi staggered on her foot. "Everyone knows we're here. Do you think people won't realize what happened? Think about it. Don't throw away your lives by getting caught up in what she's saying. She will turn on you next."

"Yes, everyone knows we're here." Harper stepped forward. "And I'll make sure they know how slippery this cove is." She raised the knife. "It was an accident. You said you were going to look for cell service, but we didn't know where you had gone. We searched for hours."

Vivi shuffled back. Small rocks fell from the edge.

Harper closed the space between them. "And when you didn't come back, we went to look for you."

Vivi suppressed a sob.

Harper looked over Vivi's shoulder. "It's so high up, isn't it? You should have known better than to stumble out here alone."

Something was missing. Harper sensed it and hesitated. She had a story, but the story only worked if everyone agreed. She turned back, an unspoken question on her thin lips.

Maria nodded. Harper cocked her head at Tessa and Steph.

Silence. But silence was complicity.

Vivi squeezed her eyes shut and blew out a shaky breath.

I bit down on my lip. She didn't deserve this. Vivi and I weren't friends. I wasn't capable of having them, and now I understood why. My leg shook. Then my whole body quivered with an internal fight between helping Vivi or saving myself. I was selfish. I would choose myself every time. That didn't make it easier to watch as Harper ran the knife down Vivi's scarred cheek.

I strained to hear sirens. "The police are coming. Just hold on," I muttered, cowardly sinking deeper into the trees.

No one was going to save her. It was too quiet... and too late for Harper to see reason. There was no more ground, and Vivi knew it. Inches away from the edge, she raised her head. Her body loosened, and she aimed a chilling glare at her friends. They had sentenced her to death, and she wouldn't let them forget it. Her expression burned into my mind. A calm had taken over her, and the edges of her lips began to rise.

Harper lunged. Vivi flew back. The edge gave out beneath her, and she fell into darkness.

TEN

My lips clamped down on the primal scream tearing through my chest. My brain fired signals my body refused to obey. Every muscle froze, forcing me to watch the scene ahead. Everyone was still. I didn't know how they didn't hear my rasping breaths.

Harper peered over the edge of the cliff. Her hair, so much like Vivi's, flapped in the wind.

"I-Is she d-dead?" Tessa's voice shook. Her voice carried despite the trembling hand clamped over her mouth.

The sight below had captivated Harper. She held a balled fist behind her, craning her neck, and walked along the edge, away from where Vivi had fallen. She crouched. She wouldn't be able to make out much in the darkness.

Maria backed away then swung round and broke into a run.

This seemed to wake Harper. Her head snapped around. "Maria."

She didn't stop. Maria leaped over the rocks, her feet

pounding the broken earth until it became soil, and branches snapped as she headed straight.

I held my breath, sure that she saw me. Then she turned. There was no path, just a cluster of bushes. She threw herself among them and surrendered to the black.

Harper raised her balled fists, clenching the knife tightly. I wondered what was going through her mind. She couldn't afford for Maria to get away. She couldn't trust her, and since she had slashed Vivi's tires, Maria's car was the only way to escape.

Harper jumped up, taking only one step forward before I saw realization dawn on her face. Maria wasn't the weakest link.

"We need to check on Vivi." Steph moved forward. "Let her go."

Harper flicked the knife. "You don't want to see that."

"Harper." Tessa choked back a sob. "Is she dead?"

"There's nothing we can do for her now."

Steph clawed at her chest. "You killed her?"

Tessa dropped to her knees, hand clamped over her mouth, and tears lined her cheeks. "No. No." She shook her head. "She could be all right. She just needs our help." Tessa staggered to her feet. Long, determined strides carried her closer to the edge until Harper's voice cut through her.

"I said she's gone."

"You don't know that," Tessa said, but she didn't attempt to get closer.

"Even if she isn't dead. What exactly are you going to do? An ambulance would never get here in time. And if they did, and she survived, think about the story she would tell. I couldn't have done it alone."

Tessa's lips trembled. "But I didn't. I wouldn—"

"You didn't stop it. Do you expect the police to believe that you weren't involved?"

Tessa's chin sank to her chest.

"I didn't push her," Harper said. "She injured herself walking around the forest and accidentally stumbled over the edge. We went out to look for her because she told us this is where anyone should go if anything happened."

Steph shook her head. "You might not have pushed her, but you gave her no choice."

"And now I'm giving you one. We catch up with Maria and leave." Harper brandished the knife. "Or I'll help you down to check on Vivi yourselves."

Tessa's chin quivered. Steph straightened her back, but defeat was apparent in her eyes as she stared into the nothingness Vivi had fallen into. Tessa didn't look up as she stepped aside, allowing Harper to walk between them and lead them away.

I waited, my mind racing and my heart pounding. They followed the route Maria had taken, arms raised as they forced their way through high branches.

Where would they go? To the car? It was likely Maria would already be there, but Jamie or the police could be there too. With no service, I wouldn't know, and the lodge wasn't safe. I wasn't going to risk running into any of the girls. Not that they knew it yet, but everyone here had a reason to keep me quiet.

There was one more place to go. My heartbeat rushed in my ears. *What if she survived?* Harper didn't seem sure, and

I couldn't leave her to bleed out at the bottom of the cove. My chest tightened. My whole body tensed. I took a deep breath and walked out.

Everything lay in darkness. The waves crashed along the shoreline then retreated slowly, washing away rocks and waste. I leaned over the edge. The wind cast moving shapes and shadows below. Among discarded towels, bottles, and beach balls, there was one undeniably different from the rest. The shape was too humanlike and unmoving despite the efforts of the wind.

My heart beat faster as I moved down the cove, clutching my stomach. The air changed, dense and heavy with salt. I leaned back, losing my footing, and skidded down the steep incline. Rough, weathered stones grated against my skin. I winced, scrambling to my feet, and followed the rest of the path to surface level. My chest tightened with every step, but no one would return for Vivi. The safest place for me now was with the dead.

Sweat lined my forehead as my feet met the sand and pebbles. The shapes I saw from above had features. A bottle filled with sand rolled in with the tide. I walked across, closer to where Vivi had fallen. A chill ran down my spine.

Mom was a nurse, and we'd played doctors and nurses when I was younger. She would lie on the floor and play dead, refusing to come back to life until I could answer the questions about what she had taught me correctly. If I got three wrong, she would flatline. It was easier to practice on my sister. All it took was a kiss on her forehead to make her better. My stomach lurched, and the contents rose to the surface.

Nothing I could do would make Vivi better. Her leg

was crushed under her, and the other lay at an unnatural angle. It felt wrong to see her drained of life. Eyes empty. No fear. No anger. Blood pooled beneath her, almost black in the moonlight. I walked around it, careful not to make contact.

"I'm sorry." I leaned over. "I wanted to help."

The silence felt like a weight. Empty eyes now held judgment. I wondered what she would have done if I were in her position. I imagined her running out to stop Harper, then the two of us at the bottom. Maybe it was to make myself feel better. Maybe I could have done more, but at least I was still here to make sure she got justice.

I couldn't save Vivi, but I would learn from her. I chewed my lip, readying myself for the ascent, but something caught my eye. A silver bracelet glittered beside her. I picked it up and wiped off as much blood as I could. It was beautiful. I hadn't taken the time before to admire the beauty in its simplicity. I pushed it into my pocket. Vivi was dead. She would have wanted me to have it.

Finding the entrance to Brittles Cove was easier once I knew what to look for. The path was more trodden and the trees thinner. But in the end, all I had to follow were the voices. I moved slowly, my knees hitched, and energy drained from my body the closer I got. Harper's voice rang through the air.

Maria's car was gone. Harper and Steph leaned on the hood of Vivi's car. Tessa crouched on the ground, her cell phone pressed to her ear.

"Try again," Steph demanded, scraping her fingers through her hair.

"I'm trying," Tessa wailed, squeezing her eyes shut.

"Give it to me." Harper snatched her cell phone. "Maria, turn back as soon as you hear this. We need to get out of here. Do you hear me?"

"Great. She is definitely going to come back now." Steph groaned. "Are you sure Vivi's keys weren't there?"

Tessa nodded.

Harper seemed almost unfazed by the fact she was responsible for the death of her friend. "She must have had them on her." She cocked her head, a faraway look on her face.

"We're not going back there," Tessa sobbed.

"We have to get out of here," Harper hissed.

Headlights in the distance closed in on us, stretching the girls' shadows. I crouched and attempted to get a better view. It wasn't a police car, but the light was too blinding to get a good look.

They pushed off the hood. Harper pulled at her waistband and slid the knife under her sweater.

They shielded their eyes as the car grew closer. One, upon a closer look, I recognized all too well. Relief flooded through me, almost bringing me to my knees. The car came to a stop, and Jamie stepped out.

For a moment, no one spoke.

"Hey." Jamie nodded, shutting the car door behind him. "Where's Dani?"

The girls exchanged uncomfortable glances.

"She called you?" Harper asked.

Jamie nodded, scanning the area. "Where is she?"

I wrestled with the idea of running out and seeing how fast we could get away. Jamie wouldn't leave without me, but I couldn't go with the girls still here.

"What did she say?" Harper's voice darkened.

"That she needed a ride. I haven't been able to get through to her since, and she sounded..." Jamie hesitated. "Where is s—"

"She's already gone." Harper stepped forward. "She left with Maria."

Jamie blinked. "Why? What happened?"

Harper ignored him, already picking up the bags at her feet and rounding Jamie's car. "We still need a ride."

Tessa and Steph scrambled behind her. Harper pulled at the car handle.

Jamie smirked. "I didn't agree to take you back."

Harper threw her things to the ground. "You can't just leave me here."

"I came for my girlfriend. You can ride with Vivi." He looked over at the black Audi.

"Please." Tears rolled down Tessa's cheeks.

Jamie grimaced. "Dani wouldn't leave without me." He rubbed his chin. "Let me try calling again."

The girls glanced at each other. My body flashed cold. Jamie pressed the cell phone to his ear.

I scrambled to my pocket, my heart racing. My mouth dry. There was no time. I couldn't make it.

Ringing erupted from my pocket.

ELEVEN

A shrill buzz pierced the air. My cell phone vibrated as I stabbed a clammy finger at the screen. The sound stopped, but it was too late.

"Dani?" Jamie called.

I bit down on my lip. My rock-hard stomach clenched. My fists squeezed by my side as I straightened and took a step forward.

They didn't know. I had been gone for almost two hours. In that time, none of them had seen me. They would assume I was at the lodge. But they had gone back to get their bags. When they didn't see me there, they would have been suspicious. My mind raced with a flurry of possible plans. If I could delay everyone leaving, the police would have time to get here. Or if Jamie and I could somehow go without the rest of them, they would have no way back.

I took a deep breath and walked out. My skin burned from the heat of their stares.

Harper's eyes searched mine. I wanted to lower my head. I was scared that if she looked long enough, she would see the truth. But this was what I was good at—keeping secrets. I would make sure they all paid, but there was value in picking the right moments.

I pulled back my shoulders and managed to form a smirk. "I see I'm not the only one who's not having fun," I said, never slowing my pace to the car.

"I thought you said she had left," Jamie said.

"Where have you been?" Harper asked, abandoning her bags by the car and stepping into my path. Up close, her eyes were darker than usual. Vivi had no chance. Small cuts lined Harper's face. Her skin was stained with dirt. Other than that, there were no signs she had just taken a life.

I shrugged. "My stomach hurt, and I remembered why I hated you all."

Steph looked up. I expected her to gloat, but she bit her lip.

Tessa looked broken, hands wrung together, eyes glassy. She needed to pull it together. We were all in trouble if Harper decided any of us could be a problem.

"I went to walk it off, and then I got lost. I managed to find service, so I called for Jamie. I think I'd prefer to be back at The Bells." My voice didn't sound like my own. I stared directly ahead, afraid any movement would lead to Harper's waist, where I knew the knife was hidden.

"Why are you guys here?" I looked down at their bags. Vivi's case was tucked behind Harper. I shifted my gaze.

"We've had enough. Like you. We would much rather be at The Bells. It's a shame we didn't even see the cove."

Something roared in my ears, and I fought hard to suppress it. "Jamie, let's go." I rounded my way to his car.

The girls looked at each other.

"We need a ride." Harper moved until she was leaning on the hood of Jamie's car.

I huffed. "You came with Maria."

Harper waved to the empty space. "As you can see, Maria and her car have gone."

Jamie sighed. "And where's Vivi?"

I bit my cheek.

"She went with Maria," Harper said.

Jamie's brows furrowed.

I swallowed, my eyes wide. *Don't question anything. Accept it.* I moved, my fingers pulling on the handle of Jamie's car. *Locked.*

Jamie pointed to the black car. "Isn't this her car?"

Harper glanced at it as though seeing it for the first time, mouth agape and eyes wide. "Yeah, she must have been in a rush."

Jamie looked at me, waiting for me to call Harper out on one of the worst lies I'd ever heard. I was willing to keep my mouth shut. The least she could do was help me.

I tugged the handle again.

Jamie drew his head back. His lips parted. If he was going to get himself stabbed, I needed another option. Could I be quick enough to get his keys and drive off without any of them stopping me?

I yanked at the door handle. "Jamie, the car."

He pressed the key and unlocked the door. "Wait."

I froze. My heart stilled.

He pointed at the deflated wheel. "She's got a flat."

There had been haircuts he'd failed to notice, but today was the day he decided to be observant. "That's probably why she went with Maria," I offered.

It was unlike me. I was too agreeable. Harper sensed it too. Her eyes never left me as I lowered myself into the passenger seat.

"You guys can get in. Put your things in the back and scrape any mud off your boots," Jamie said before getting into the driver's seat and unlocking the trunk.

He leaned in, and I flinched. "Where's all your stuff?"

"It doesn't matter," I managed under my breath. "Let's just get back."

He stared for a moment, a hand on my lap. "Is everything okay?"

I pulled my seat belt over me. "I just want to go."

"What happened?"

I parted my lips, but we were no longer alone in the car. The girls clambered into the backseat. Harper was the last one in, carefully shifting and shielding her waistband. She didn't bother with her seat belt, leaning to hiss in a trembling Tessa's ear.

Something sounded in the distance, out of place among the rustle of the leaves and the quiet of the forest. No one else seemed to notice. The engine roared, and anger boiled in my chest.

We pulled away from the lodge, away from Vivi. My heart clenched. They didn't deserve to get away with this.

"Thank you, Jamie." Tessa's voice was different—high pitched and quivering. "It's nice of you to come and pick us up."

The car beeped, and a light flashed on the dashboard. Jamie huffed, taking both hands off the steering wheel to put on his seat belt. "I didn't realize the rest of you were leaving."

I relaxed slightly when no one replied, but my body tensed as Jamie touched my knee.

"Dani." Harper's voice cut through me. I could feel her breath on the back of my neck. "What happened to you while we were gone?"

A sudden, overwhelming feeling of dread rushed through me. I cleared my throat. "What are you talking about?"

"The blood."

I didn't turn to face Harper or look down at my knee. I didn't have to. I knew what she was talking about—the dark patch on the material on my pants. Vivi's blood.

"Did something happen?" Jamie asked.

I swallowed. "Just focus on the road."

"Did something happen?" Harper echoed.

Adrenaline shot through my system. We were moving. I just needed to get back to The Bells, and then I could find help.

I blew out a breath with confidence I didn't have. "Why don't you ask Steph?"

Harper had moved again. I could no longer feel her at the back of my neck.

"She's lying," Steph said. "I didn't hit her that hard. She wasn't bleeding when I left."

"You hit her?" Jamie glanced in the rearview mirror, his hands tightening around the steering wheel.

I gritted my teeth. "Just keep driving."

"Why are you in such a rush to get away?" Harper asked calmly.

I swallowed. "I could ask you the same question."

"Dani, what happened?" Jamie asked. The car swerved

as he avoided a low-hanging branch at the last second. Jamie had one hand on the wheel. The other pushed Harper back as she forced her way through the gap between the driver and passenger seat.

"What do you think you're doing?" Jamie asked.

Harper didn't seem to hear. "I think you went to the cove and saw something you shouldn't have." She peered down at me. "And you, being Dani, couldn't help but involve yourself in things that have nothing to do with you. It's her blood? Isn't it?"

"What are you talking about?" Jamie asked.

I took in a deep breath. We hadn't made it far and were still surrounded by woodland and darkness. Nowhere to call for help.

"What did you see, Dani?" she hissed. Spit flew onto my cheek.

I met her eyes seething with anger.

Tessa whimpered in the back.

Confined between the two front seats, Harper couldn't reach for the knife. Tessa and Steph only went along with her out of fear. Now she was outnumbered. She couldn't kill all of us. One might have to be used as a sacrifice, which was perfect because Steph was here.

I leaned in, remembering Vivi's vacant stare. They didn't even check to see if she was breathing. As far as they knew, Vivi was still at the bottom, dying slowly. I braced myself. Dread became fury.

"You killed her!" I screamed.

"No." Tessa sobbed uncontrollably.

Harper lunged forward. I tensed, waiting for the hit. It didn't come.

She snatched at the wheel, fighting Jamie for control. The car swerved, and a thick trunk towered over us. My whole body reacted, bracing for the impact. I was thrown forward. The airbag deployed, cushioning the blow.

First, I registered the clunk of the metal. The hood of the wrecked car hissed, and acrid smoke filled the air. Heat lashed against my chest—the seat belt throwing me back. Shards of glass shimmered in the light, and a cruel wind swept through the car.

Someone in the back screamed, but I couldn't turn my neck. My stomach crunched. I silently thanked the seat belt, and hope rose in my chest. The only person not wearing a seat belt was Harper, who'd been thrown headfirst into the windshield. She lay still on the dashboard. There was a beat where I thought she was dead, and a mix of emotions raced through me. I didn't know if I was ready to see two dead bodies in one night, but if it had to be her, I could live with it.

Then she pulled back. Blood was smeared around her mouth. A long gash ran along her forehead. Her hand gripped around my wrist. "If we let you leave, our lives are over."

TWELVE

I hunched over. The sharp pain in my ribs was worse than anything I had felt before. I took in a breath. I was in pain but alive. My body relaxed, but something was wrong. As tension eased, and something else tightened. A voice snarled. Pain seared from the viselike grip on my wrist. I looked up and tugged, trying to free myself from Harper's grasp.

She seethed, caught between two deflating airbags, her muscles straining against her bloodstained skin, lips pulled back against her teeth.

A wail rang in my head. *Is she screaming? No.* The sound was coming from behind. *Tessa? Steph?*

"Dani?" Jamie groaned.

I didn't turn. My mind was racing. My free hand jabbed at the seat belt buckle. It came free.

Harper's eyes widened in surprise. I moved quickly, thrusting my free hand into her face. She let go and cupped her nose.

I pushed open the door. My feet barely touched the

ground before I was yanked back. Harper held a fistful of my hair and growled as she pulled. My scalp burned. Tears blurred my vision. The sound of strands ripping echoed in my head. I swung wildly, catching something, or someone. Then I fell headfirst out of the car.

I scrambled across the ground. The temperature had dropped. The air felt sharp. Ice prickled against bone. Jamie had Harper locked in a hold. Glass shards sprinkled from her hair. The car's metal twisted against the tree.

Tessa was out cold, her head slumped against the window. Steph moved, shrieking, as she fought against the restraints of her seat belt.

Harper roared. She threw her head back, colliding with Jamie's. She broke out of his hold and climbed out through the front window, broken glass grating against her legs. Jamie grabbed her by the leg. Harper kicked, catching Jamie in the neck, and he let go. Harper staggered into the tree trunk, pulled herself up, and jumped down from the hood, blood pouring from her forehead.

"Dani!" Jamie screamed. He threw open the car door and fell out. "Are you okay?"

My throat caught. My head throbbed. The world seemed to spin. Harper was a blur, stumbling forward. Something glinted in her hand. I tried to focus, but dark spots clouded my vision, and my heart rattled against my ribcage.

My muscles tensed. My legs trembled. In the situation of fight or flight, my body froze. My feet rooted in place. My heart threatened to rip out of my chest.

"You don't know how long I've wanted to do this." It

was Harper's voice, but I couldn't tell where it had come from.

There was another figure, tall and slender.

I couldn't move my lips. But it was okay because Steph was coming to help. I blinked. Things started to come back into focus. Harper moved closer, but Steph didn't. She got smaller.

Something in my stomach sank. She was running away. I couldn't complain. I deserved it. It was what I'd done to Vivi.

Was this what she went through? Tears brimmed my eyes. My life flashed before me. I wanted to remember my happy moments and my family, but all I got were regrets. Not using the secrets I knew to my advantage. Not leaving The Bells when I had the chance. Allowing these girls to get close enough to hurt me.

Harper grinned wildly.

I squeezed my eyes shut. Tears rolled down my cheek. "I'm sorry." I blew out a shaky breath. Everything heightened as I waited for the end.

It didn't come.

Grunting echoed. I opened my eyes. Harper was on the floor, arms pinned down by Jamie. She struggled, still clutching the knife.

"Run," Jamie called.

I didn't move. I wheezed hard and fast.

"Dani?" Jamie groaned.

I took a step backward. "I'm here."

"Run," he ordered, turning to look over his shoulder, giving Harper the space she needed to free her hands.

Jamie realized a second too late. Harper had already

begun to swing. The knife caught Jamie's side, and he fell onto Harper.

"Run," he grunted.

I did, not looking back. My heart was racing, and my feet were barely touching the ground. If I had a signal, I could call for help. I needed to get back to Vivi's car.

Something grew for Jamie. Love? Admiration? Or maybe the realization that I still had a use for him.

I kept running. I couldn't hear Harper or Jamie anymore. Branches snapped beneath me. My breath rang in my head. Then I froze.

It was quiet, but I heard it. Something wailed in the distance. I kept moving, holding my breath, until it became clearer. Sirens.

I exhaled, my hand clenching my chest. "Here!" I screamed, the cry ripping through my chest.

I fell to the ground, sucking in breaths. I was also calling Harper to where I was, but if there was a chance help was coming, I had to risk it.

"Here." It took everything I had to cry out. I tried to catch my breath, but my throat closed in on itself. "I'm here," I sobbed.

Red and blue flashes lit up the sky. I almost passed out when two officers stepped out of the police car.

A short-haired man walked toward me. "Are you hurt? What's happened?"

Heat rose to the back of my eyes. "Vivi's dead. They killed her."

Police tape flapped in the wind, lighting up in flashes as the crime scene photographer studied the area. I shielded my face. The shock of light illuminated the wrecked car and the bloody knife on the ground. I couldn't stop shaking. I tried to focus on the murmurs of the police radio. They had gone to look for Vivi, racing against the tide.

Jamie blew out a breath, tugging the foil wrapper around me before placing his arm around me. For the first time in months, I leaned into him.

"They won't find anything in the car," he whispered to himself.

I didn't know what he meant. I didn't want to.

His head was stained with red. He wiped the blood with his forearm then pressed it against the side of his torso. Harper had slashed him, but it wasn't deep enough to be life-threatening. Jamie refused to get checked until he could be sure I was okay.

I wasn't okay. My eyes narrowed as the police interviewed Steph. I couldn't hear what she was saying, but I could practically see the lies on her lips.

"Hey." Jamie pulled back. "I'm so glad you called me. I would do anything for you, Dani. I don't know what I would have done if—" He sniffed.

I hadn't seen this much emotion from him in years. I swallowed the lump in my throat. "I'm okay."

"It's funny. I think this is the closest we've been. It only took nearly dying to get here."

We laughed, realized we both had sustained severe damage to our ribs, and tried to control the increased laughter.

Jamie pulled his hand away from his side, and blood coated his palm.

I didn't trust anyone. I was used to doing everything alone, but Jamie threw himself in front of a knife for me. It showed that I could change. Having the right person who loved and trusted me could be as powerful as keeping secrets.

I looked up at Jamie. He would do for now. He had potential but lacked competency. "You need to get checked out," I said.

"I know you want to do it by yourself. I know how strong you are, but remember to lean on me. I am always here for you."

"I know. And when we get back to campus, maybe I'll move some of my things into yours."

He smiled. "Good. Then I can always protect you."

I wanted safety, a life where there was nothing I needed protection from. Vivi's death had started with a series of mistakes. The first one was her choice of friends.

Maria had escaped. Harper would say anything but the truth. Steph and Tessa would turn against each other, and Vivi wasn't here to tell her story. But I was.

They all had something to gain from Vivi's death, and I realized I did too. I tightened the foil sheet around me as the officer approached. My ribs were bruised, and everything ached.

"Miss Bishop, we would like to interview you now."

Jamie didn't move.

"It's okay," I whispered.

His jaw tensed, but he nodded and went to be checked by the emergency services.

The officer took the seat beside me. "Can you take me through what happened today?"

I wrung my fingers and nodded. "They all planned it. Maria, Harper, Tessa, and Steph. But it was mainly Steph's idea." I coughed roughly. My version of events would be enough to get Vivi justice. It didn't have to be true.

I broke into a series of coughs, and the officer signaled for someone to get water. I sucked in a breath. "Did they find Vivi?"

The officer nodded.

"She didn't deserve this. She was scared. She wanted to leave, but Harper slashed her car tires. Then Steph lured her to the cove. They all stood by the edge, closing in on her until she fell."

"Are you sure?"

I wet my lips and nodded. "I saw it all. They wanted Vivi to agree to restart their business together, and when she refused—" I shook my head. "I just wish I could have helped her. Maria escaped. She left in her car."

"Don't worry. We have officers in the area on the lookout."

"What will happen to the rest of the girls?"

"We can't say for sure right now."

I ran through everything that had happened, careful to spread the blame equally among the girls. Harper wasn't the only one at fault, and this was my opportunity to get rid of all of them.

Officers marched them past. Harper strained against handcuffs, her bandaged forehead soaked with blood. She lashed out at her accompanying officer, screaming and swearing as she was dragged to a police car.

Tessa followed, her head low, shadows obscuring her expression. She would get the fame she always wanted, just not for the right reasons.

Steph walked behind her. Her body was wracked with sobs, and tears raced down her cheeks, almost enough to swim in. I couldn't help but smile.

I wasn't being led away in handcuffs or dead at the bottom of the cove. Tonight, I had survived death. Would I have done anything differently? If I had known, it wouldn't be long before it came to claim me.

DEAR READER

Thank you for taking the time to read *Secrets of the Dead*. It has been an amazing journey bringing these characters to life, and I am grateful for your support. If you enjoyed this book, please consider leaving a review.

The story continues in *Our Secrets Die With Her...*

OUR
SECRETS
DIE
WITH HER
SIMBI FEYISARA

ONE

A wail of sirens pierced the room. Flashes of red and blue illuminated the walls, casting shadows across the pale, lifeless figure slumped on the bed opposite me. Sunken eyes bore into the ceiling, unmoving. Then they blinked—because Dani wasn't dead. I just wished she was.

The walls pulsed; music and jeers clashed with the sirens. The dorm room filled with the scent of a house party—traces of sweat and vomit. I had planned to be out of The Bells before the party started, but there was one thing I couldn't leave without—my cell phone. I turned my back to Dani to lift my pillows and pull back the duvet. I didn't think it would miraculously appear, but I had already checked the bathroom and every corner of our dorm room. Well, I hadn't looked through Dani's side, but there weren't many hiding places. In fact, there were fewer than usual. Gone were Dani's photos, candles, and fairy lights. She had no study books. I doubted if she had opened a book or done an assignment herself. She had people to do them for her. Only her gold swimming trophies and medals remained, bundled under her desk, along with a few hair products scattered on top. And although the bruise was fading, looking at the chipped wood on the white matte finish, I still felt the soreness on my hip from my latest attempt to take back the clothes she had stolen. Today, I'd been forced to wear a mocha-colored dress a few shades lighter than my skin.

I dropped my bedding and took a sharp breath as my eyes roamed to Dani's closet. A bathrobe hung off the door, obscuring the contents, my clothes likely among them. I could picture my cell phone there. I stepped toward it.

Dani turned to face me, smiling as smooth brown hair fell on her face, the strands almost instinctively avoiding her eyes. Green irises trailed me around the room, as they always did, wide-eyed and looking for secrets. It was how Dani knew my cell's four-digit PIN and how she'd managed to go through my messages, contacts, and photos. She had never admitted to it, but it was the only way she could know the things she did.

I had a clear recollection of placing my cell phone on the bed. I lifted the sheets once more, and Dani's gaze followed. I bit down on my lip, accepting that I would have to leave without my cell phone. I made my bed, angling pillows and tucking in sheets. I had no intention of coming back if things went well tonight. I picked up my jacket folded over my desk chair.

The sirens stopped. Screams and laughter grew louder, and the smell of smoke mixed in the stagnant air. Dani leaped up and stepped onto my bed, ruffling my freshly made sheets and toppling my carefully stacked pillows to the floor. She climbed onto my desk and rested a knee and dirty sneaker on my study notes. She leaned out the window, and I fought the urge to shove her out of it. I scoffed, gesturing to the perfectly functional window on her side of the room, but she didn't notice. She didn't even open it, coughing heavily into the crook of her elbow before her deep-set eyes tracked movement below, neck craned, and shoulders hunched.

I took the chance. My body was drawn to Dani's side of the room. I moved cautiously, making sure Dani was still perched on the windowsill. I pulled back her cover, exposing wrinkled sheets that didn't quite reach the edge of the mattress. A slip of paper peeked out from beneath the corner of her pillow. *Sherwood Station* was written in bold for two out-of-state tickets tonight. No return. My hands instinctively reached for the tickets. Then the silver case of my cell phone caught my eye.

Heat surged through my body. Dani had watched me search for half an hour while leaning on the very thing I needed. I tapped the screen awake. Blocked, with one minute remaining. At least she hadn't worked out the new passcode, but now her smile had a new meaning.

"Dani," I called, a sharp edge in my voice.

She didn't move, her lips a thin line. Her skin was tinged red. Her glazed eyes were focused on something outside. I stepped toward her, my cell phone clutched in my hand.

She started. In a swift motion, she jumped down from the desk, pulling the blue tartan curtain closed. The room darkened. Her cheeks were flushed, and sweat lined her forehead. She looked at the cell phone and smiled, her teeth gleaming. Dani cocked her head. "You changed your passcode."

Rage brewed in the pit of my stomach. She wanted a reaction. Every part of me screamed to give her one.

"Sienna, you should know better than to leave things lying around." Dani's eyes were wide with amusement. She stepped slowly toward me as she returned to her side of the room. She wiped her forehead and leaned back on her bed.

I ignored her. My head was pounding from the heat. I walked to the window and reached for the curtain.

"Leave it closed." Dani was propped up on her elbow, an unusual note of panic in her voice. "Please."

I wanted to rip open the curtains to spite her, but I held my arm there. "What's gotten into you?"

"Nausea." She settled back into the bed, massaging two fingers against her temple, and forced a lazy smile. "I'm sure it'll pass once you leave." She pulled her pillow forward, obscuring the tickets.

"Looks like you're the one going somewhere."

She leaned back against the pillow. "You know, I've always admired your wishful thinking."

I dropped my hand, took my jacket, and angled my cell phone out of view as I typed in my passcode, earning a smile from Dani.

The screen flashed with a message from Tyrell: *Am I supposed to believe it's only a coincidence you're late when I pick the movie?*

I couldn't contain the smile that spread as I clicked to respond.

"So, that's still going on," Dani remarked. "That explains where you were last night."

I slid the cell phone into my pocket. "I don't know what you're talking about."

Dani didn't bite. She pulled a blue gym bag from under her bed. "Oh yeah. You can have back those clothes you lent me."

I looked at the ceiling, taking a deep breath, before walking over to retrieve the pile of clothes Dani had stolen. I inspected them, threw mine into a bag, and folded the rest over my desk chair. I would find their owners later. There was another bag under Dani's bed. Half open, it held bundles of sweaters, dresses, and skirts. Some were rolled and tucked in neatly; others looked as though they had been thrown in. Dani followed my gaze and kicked the bag farther beneath her bed.

"Don't worry. None of it's yours." She squinted, her eyes lit with a twinkle of mischief. The door rattled, and the look of amusement quickly disappeared from her face.

"What's up with the door?" I asked, moving toward it.

Dani wiped at the sweat on her forehead. "I locked it."

As my biggest threat was already living in the room with me, I had never taken to locking the door, and neither had Dani, until today.

"Dani, I know you're in there."

I rolled my eyes at the familiar shrill voice, unlocked the door, and let it swing open.

Our housemate, Ainsley, stood there with a hand on her hip, her thick braids cascading over one shoulder, her dark skin covered in shimmering gold makeup. The air was thicker. In the dim haze behind her, bodies packed the hallway, singing loudly.

Ainsley wedged a foot in the gap. "Where are you going?" She scanned my outfit with disgust.

"The choices were between this party and Dani, so I've found something better to do."

Dani scoffed, a newfound confidence in her tone. "I still think you could aim higher, Monroe."

My body stiffened, the way it always did when I heard that name. I swallowed quickly, lowering my head and stepping back to let Ainsley in. The weight of two pairs of eyes on me was heavy. Ainsley's sparkled with recognition. She knew Dani was playing with a secret.

There was a sudden roar from the party—the guests were seemingly impressed with the DJ's latest offering—but the silence here was deafening.

Ainsley still stood by the threshold, impatience etched on her face. She stepped aside. "Get out."

I took my bag with my clothes. "Only since you asked so nicely," I muttered and passed. If it was strange that Ainsley was kicking me out of my own room, I didn't care. In the stuffy air of the hall, I glanced back at Dani. Something haunting was in her expression. Shoulders back, chest out, she held that familiar playful grin. Then Ainsley kicked the door shut, rattling the bronzed number four.

The four dorm rooms of The Bells were confined to a single rectangular hallway, with one room on each side of the walls. The common room was on the left, and the kitchen was on the right. People I had never seen before flowed between the rooms, dancing and singing. At the back, next to my dorm room, was a small utility room. I opened the door and dropped my clothes inside before weaving through bodies in the hall. I had never been to a party at Stedmond, and it didn't fill me with confidence that Ainsley had shared the entrance key code to The Bells with half the campus.

I made it to the lobby, where the air was lighter because the door was propped open by a fire extinguisher. Its contents had been fired over an unsuspecting victim, who was passed out on one of the plush chairs.

I stepped into the cold and shrugged on my jacket. The police car was gone. The police had been regular visitors at The Bells since the death of Alex, a student from Stedmond, had forced the college to at least look as though they were taking the war on drugs seriously.

"Hey, Sienna." Bianca, one of my roommates, was climbing the steps to the entrance. She was still in her gym clothes. Her deep-brown curls were damp, and the faint smell of chlorine lingered on her. Even if she wasn't just coming from swim practice, something told me she would have looked out of place at this party. "Have you seen Ainsley?" She folded her arms across her chest. "I wanted her to do something about the noise."

"Good luck." I held back a laugh and hoped for her sake the music couldn't get any louder. "She's in my room with Dani."

"Dani?" She blinked, arms tightening around her. "Is she feeling better? She said she was too ill to go practice."

Dani was the best on the swim team. But talent didn't equal likability. Her flu was probably the best thing that had happened to the team in a while.

"Don't worry, you still have a bit longer without her."

Bianca blushed. "No, I didn't mean—" She shook her head. "Are you staying?"

"As tempting as that sounds... I have already made plans."

Bianca swallowed. "Okay, then I'll see you later."

Stedmond College was once a prestigious institution, but now it was plagued with drugs, cheating, and death. Pathways connected the various facilities, main buildings, and residential areas. The Bells was on the edge of campus.

I walked down the steps and through the parking lot. Streetlights towered the usually deserted parking lot. Crushed soda cans and cigarette butts lined the ground. As I waded through the narrow rows, I heard the thunk of a car door hitting another, then an alarm filled the air. At the edge of the parking lot, there were two routes. One pathway led farther into campus, and the second followed a dimly lit alley to Stedmond Park.

It was the light that pulled me in that direction—casting one shadow along the cracked sidewalk. I recognized the straw-like hair as belonging to Jamie, Dani's ex-boyfriend. His hands jerked, and he leaned through the open window of a silver sports car. The headlights were too bright for me to see the driver. Jamie was shouting, his jaw tense, and veins pulsed in his neck. I couldn't make out any words above the muffled noise of the party. He moved back, pulling at his hair, looking frantic. The car jerked forward, and Jamie lunged. He banged on the hood then clasped at the door handle, trying to force it open. When that didn't work, he put his arm through the window.

"Let go," I called. I was moving now, my breath hitching as my feet hit the ground.

Jamie was trying to grab something. I opened my mouth to shout to him, but I wasn't fast enough. The window flew up, trapping Jamie's arm. The car sped up, dragging him. His face reddened from the effort as he fought to free himself.

He did and smacked to the ground then tumbled. The car tires screeched, and the engine roared as it sped off. I felt the rush of wind as it passed me in a blur.

"Are you okay?" I called, crossing the street.

Jamie threw a fist on the ground. "Do I look okay?" He propped himself onto his elbow and groaned. Small scratches were carved into his reddened skin.

I paused in the middle of the darkened road. "Do you want me to call someone?"

He shook his head. I didn't know exactly who I was offering to call. Jamie didn't have friends. It was always him and Dani. They'd been inseparable... until she left him for Michael.

"What about the police?"

Irritation flashed on his face. "I fell," he said through gritted teeth, wincing as he pushed himself up. He brushed at his clothes. Blood seeped from his split lip.

"That's an interesting way of putting things."

"We both know you don't care."

"Who was in the car?"

"A friend."

"Seemed like it."

He inhaled sharply. "People fight when they care about each other. Speaking of which, how's Dani?"

"Still with Michael."

"Ouch." He threw a hand to his chest. He masked it well, but the slight clench of his jaw revealed what everyone knew. He wanted her back. "It won't last," he said confidently, looking over his shoulder at the iron gates and greenery of Stedmond Park. "I'm going to stay here. Don't let me stop you from your date."

"It's not a date." Heat rushed to my cheeks.

He laughed as I turned and walked away, the sound becoming strained as he broke into a cough.

Tyrell and I were acquaintances. I wasn't built for relationships. Tyrell was convenient for the only thing I needed—an excuse to escape The Bells. Screams and music quietened as I moved against the flow of people heading away from the center of campus. The library and main buildings were empty, with only a few lights on. The presence of security increased as I got closer to Platinum. I'd begged Mom to stay somewhere like this. Everyone had their own room, and there was a reception desk and an indoor cafeteria. Mom insisted it was important not to be isolated and to make as many friends as possible after all the unfortunate things that happened. That was how she described all my friends turning their backs on me and our neighborhood hating us. Not that I blamed them. But now I was stuck with housemates who felt the same way.

I leaned against the pole at the gates to the building and messaged Tyrell to let him know I was downstairs.

He appeared moments later, his full lips spread in a grin, his hands tucked into his bright-blue puffy jacket. "Hey. We could skip the movie tonight. I heard there's a party not to be missed on campus."

I gave him a warning look. "Not funny. Plus, I think Ainsley would combust if she saw me having fun at one of her parties."

"Now, that would be fun to see." Tyrell withdrew his

hands from his pocket, and for a moment, he paused. I thought he was going to go for a hug.

I stepped back as he gestured to the Platinum parking lot. *Not a hug.* I bit down on my lip and fell into step beside him, masking my disappointment.

"It would at least be more entertaining than robots turning into zombies?"

From the crease in Tyrell's brow, I knew this wasn't exactly the premise of the movie he'd suggested. His lips parted, and he hesitated for a moment, as if considering whether to take the bait. Then he sighed and scratched the small scar on his brow, as he always did before he went into one of his rants. "They aren't robots. They are artificial intelligence agents, and they don't turn into zombies. They—"

I covered my lips to stifle my laugh.

He raised a brow, opened his mouth, then closed it again, smiling. "I'm glad you find the apocalypse funny." He pressed his key card to the gates of the parking lot. The Bells was not important enough to have a gate. "We can watch something else if you want."

"And miss the opportunity for me to inaccurately recall everything for my own amusement?"

He held open the gate and rolled his eyes playfully.

I stepped through. "It's fine. Anything is better than being at The Bells."

The car chirped as Tyrell unlocked it. "That bad?"

"I spent half an hour looking for my cell phone, which Dani stole."

"Really? Even after the way you scared her off last week." He brushed a hand over his low fade.

I cocked my head.

He bit back a smile. "I know everyone else thinks you lost the fight, but as your—"

An unspoken word hung in the air. *Friend? Something more?* My chest tightened. I wished he had finished the sentence. I needed to know he understood that this wasn't going anywhere. It couldn't.

"I know you were just holding back." He finished quickly, ducking his head into the car before I could read his expression.

"And I have the bruises to prove it," I muttered, following his lead and entering the car.

It hadn't been much of a fight, and I'd fallen back into the desk, but according to everyone else, Dani had battered me to a pulp.

Tyrell pulled at his seat belt. "I'm glad to know Dani took your cell phone. For a while, I thought you were blowing me off."

An unsettling feeling clawed at my stomach. "No. Just Dani being Dani."

I spent two hours of the movie wishing the apocalypse would come and put me out of my misery, and fifteen minutes questioning my sanity as Tyrell raved about the movie on the way back to the parking lot. "With that ending, there will have to be a part two."

It almost sounded like a threat. "Sorry, I think I've made plans to spend the whole day with Dani."

"Well, if the movies aren't your thing," he teased.

"No, just that movie in particular. Or pretty much any of the movies you make me watch," I amended.

We weaved through a row of cars until Tyrell stopped by his. "You mean you're not hanging out with me for my love of movies?"

"No. You're lucky everything else about you is great."

He paused, running a finger through the slit in his brow.

I hadn't meant to say it aloud. I cleared my throat. "What happened to your eyebrow?"

He unlocked his car and smiled. "I was five and trying to get the last cookie. Unfortunately, so was my sister, and the dinner table was on her side."

I opened the door and entered. "You didn't get the cookie?"

"No." He put the key into the ignition. "But I got two stitches, so who's the real winner?"

"Katelyn," I said with surprising speed.

Tyrell had talked about his whole family, which also included his brother and parents, so much that it felt as though I knew them.

"You remind me of my sister sometimes."

I raised a brow. "Really? How?"

"She hates the movies I watch too. What about you? Tell me something about your family?"

I wanted to give him something, but the first memory that came to mind was the police knocking on the door. I tucked my arm against my body and sighed. "We're not as close as yours."

He opened his lips as though he wanted to ask more but thought better of it. It wasn't the first time he'd asked about my family, and answering was getting harder to avoid.

"How do you feel about the police commissioner campaign?" he asked, pulling his seat belt over himself.

I drew my head back, confused, but grateful for the change of subject. "The one Ainsley's dad is running for?"

He nodded.

I put on my seat belt. "Indifferent."

"For my next research project, I am going to follow the candidates and interview students to see how they are influenced. You up for it?"

"What would I have to do?"

"Keep up-to-date with all the latest news, and I'll interview you and other participants to see if or how your view changes as the election goes on. I'd send you different news—"

"How long would this take?"

"It would be from now until the results in a few months."

"Oh. It sounds like a great project," I said slowly, something sinking in my stomach. I'd let things get too far. Now he was making plans months from now.

"Just not one you would be interested in?"

I wet my lips. "I don't think, um… It wouldn't be a good idea. I… Maybe you could ask Jamie," I stammered. "He was by The Bells. He was arguing with someone, and they almost ran him over."

Tyrell blinked. "You can tell me if you don't want to do it."

"It's not that. It's just—"

"You don't know where we'll be a few months from now," Tyrell finished.

I kept quiet, swallowing the lump in my throat. I should

have stopped it because there could never be a future. And now he knew too. I braced myself as he parted his lips. He was going to do what I should have done a long time ago.

"I know we haven't had the discussion about us. But I just thought things were going well enough for us to plan things in the future."

He wasn't breaking things off. I expected to feel relieved, but my throat tightened. "When did you decide that?"

"It's not something I decided," he said carefully.

I bit down on my lip. When given enough time, everyone turned their back on me. When they got to know me enough, they didn't like what they saw. I wasn't going to be able to keep Tyrell at arm's length anymore.

He took a deep breath. "Things have been going well. I'm happy with us jus—"

"There is no us." I unbuckled my seat belt and scrambled for the door handle. "I'll find my own way back." I opened the door. "Good luck with your project, and thanks for everything. I appreciated the distraction."

His jaw went slack. "Distrac—" He scoffed. "Okay. So, this is the part where you push me away."

I slammed the door and heard shouts of my name. Something inside me was begging me to turn back. With every step, my heart felt like it was shrinking, which was perfect. I wasn't capable of love.

I passed through the parking lot, my feet sore from the walk in the cold. I expected to be met with a heavy stare, but there was nothing. The Bells had been deserted; only wreckage left behind. The wind picked up, amplifying the sound of clattering empty cans and bottles in the parking lot. I shifted on my feet and looked up at the drawn curtain. Sometimes, it felt like Dani could see through me. With one look, she would know something had happened with Tyrell. She wasn't there, but something was off. The curtain flapped with the wind. The window was broken, and only a few fragmented shards remained.

I quickened my pace, and a weight in my chest increased as I flew up the steps to The Bells entrance. I pulled away the fire extinguisher, and the door slammed with a heavy thud. The lobby was empty. Cold seeped into my bones, and I wrapped my arms around my middle. I walked to the hallway, and the corridor bulbs lit up overhead as I followed a trail of empty cans, bottles, and popcorn ground into the carpet. The air was a sickly mix of sweat and aftershave. The house felt different, hollow. I tightened the hold on my body in a futile attempt to stop the churning. The house was a mess because of the party.

Dani was leaving. Maybe the broken window was her parting gift, and the tightness in my chest was because of Tyrell. *I should have agreed to do his project.*

As I walked through the hall, my footsteps were the only sound. I brought out my key card, remembering how Dani had locked the door earlier, but it wasn't needed. The handle clicked, and the door swung back with ease. A small offering of light from the hall cast the room in shadows. Wind ripped through the room. Disappointment raced through me.

Dani was on the edge of her bed, not on her way out of state. The door slammed closed, and the curtain flapped, allowing through flashes of moonlight. Something was wrong. Dani didn't stir. A metallic taste filled the air.

"Dani?" My voice shook. My eyes darted around the darkness, looking for any subtle movement. I flicked the light switch, and my hand came back reddened and wet.

Light flooded the room. My body tensed. Dani lay slumped unnaturally. Her emerald eyes were vacant. Lips, normally upturned in a cunning smile, were parted and covered in blood.

I stepped back, shallow breaths coming hard and fast, but my body refused to take in any oxygen. Nausea raced through me. My whole body was numb.

Dani was dead.

TWO

"Hi, Sienna." A tall man dressed smartly in all black leaned forward onto the kitchen table and gestured to the chair opposite him.

I sat. My hands shook uncontrollably until I pushed them under my thighs.

"I am Detective Collins. I will be conducting your interview."

I nodded. The kitchen table was the only surface that looked remotely clean, but it was as though it had been wiped in a rush. Dry streaks lined the table, and a few crumbs were left in the corners surrounding a half-empty glass of water and a desk light lamp borrowed from the common room. I squinted through to see the rest of the room. Trash overflowed from the garbage can. Bloated chips and popcorn floated in the blocked sink. Shards of glass had been swept into a corner, and the bulb from the kitchen light was missing.

Collins cleared his throat. "I know it can't be easy after

what you have experienced tonight. I appreciate you talking to us."

He said it as though I had a choice. My roommates had been brought in here one after the other while I tried to understand what I had seen, wrestling with the rising panic because the police were coming for me. Well, to me. This wasn't the first time they'd wanted to speak to me in relation to a murder, but this time, Mom wasn't sitting beside me, a firm hand on my knee. The gesture had probably seemed like reassurance, like a loving mother comforting her daughter. Only I had noticed as she squeezed and pinched when my answers weren't good enough or I wasn't sticking to the story. She always said that the police were the reason for our broken family. I never disagreed because the alternative would be to blame me. Strangely, I wished she was here so I didn't have to go through this alone.

"This is my partner, Detective Shelley." Collins gestured to the narrow-nosed woman beside him. A couple of hours ago, she had collected my clothes and offered me something to change into, a small act of kindness as the bloody brown cotton clung to my body and burned my skin. We didn't speak, but her presence was the reminder I needed that all of this was real. Having her here now should have been calming, but her smile didn't quite reach her eyes.

"Hi," I breathed, my gaze focused on the table. They felt too close, their sharp eyes too invasive. I took a deep breath, my heart rattling in my chest as I pushed back. A screech filled the air as the legs of my chair scraped along the floor tiles.

Collins raised a brow, searching my face.

"Sorry," I muttered, gazing at the window. I was about to ask the detectives to open it when Collins spoke.

"I understand that you were the person who found Dani and called the ambulance." He clicked his pen, and his hand clasped around a notepad angled out of view.

I fought the urge to crane my neck and nodded.

"And when did you last see Dani?"

I swallowed. "Before I left, around ten, she was in bed. In my roo—our room," I amended quickly.

Collins made a note of something. "And how did she seem?"

I thought about that for a moment. It didn't seem like the time to mention that Dani was up to her usual tricks and had stolen my phone or that we'd had another of our many disagreements. "Normal."

"What constitutes as normal for Dani?"

I tried to wet my lips, my mouth dry. "She was lying in bed, avoiding the party."

"And where were you between ten and five?" He clicked the tip of his pen against his lips.

I swallowed hard. "I went to watch a movie, and then I went for a walk."

Another note. "And is there anyone else who can verify your story?"

I squeezed my fingers around my thighs. I had already decided I was going to leave Tyrell out of it. He didn't deserve to be interrogated or involved in any of this. I knew how the police could twist things. My chest tightened as I remembered his face when I walked away. "No," I croaked. "I went alone. I still have the ticket in my jacket if you need to see it."

"Okay," he said in a low voice and scribbled in his notepad. I looked to Detective Shelley. Her arms were folded over her stomach, and her eyes unwavering. Did she doubt what I was saying?

My throat felt uncomfortably dry. I grabbed the glass on the table with a shaky hand. I wasn't sure if it was for me or one of my housemates who'd been interviewed before me, but I gulped down the stale water.

Collins cleared his throat. "Did you speak to Dani before you left?"

"No. Not really. I was hardly in the room."

"Hmm." He breathed into his pen and lowered it to his lips.

I braced myself for the click, but he pulled away. "And when you were in the room, what did the two of you talk about?"

I pulled at the neckline of my dress. "Umm, she gave me some of my clothes that she had sto—borrowed. I left them in the utility room before I left." I remembered how much everything had changed only a few hours ago.

Dani had been as nosy and evasive as always. She knew everything about everyone while revealing nothing about herself. But there was something different about the way she'd acted. "I think she was leaving," I said. "She had two tickets for out of state under her pillow and a bag packed under her bed. When I tried to ask her about it, she didn't answer."

Collins hummed under his breath, and I tried to remember if the bag was there when I came back.

"Was that unusual behavior for Dani?"

"No. She only ever left The Bells to stay with her boyfriend."

"And who is that?"

"Michael. I don't know his last name. But he goes to Stedmond, as well."

"Did Michael ever come to The Bells?"

"Sometimes he would sneak in but never stayed the night."

"Sneak?" Collins asked.

Heat flushed the back of my neck. "Yes. He's an ex of Nia, one of our housemates."

Collins noted something down. I didn't mention the overlap between the two relationships, and while Michael may have sneaked, Dani wasn't half as considerate.

"How was Dani when you left?"

"She was fine. Ainsley came and said she wanted to talk to Dani in private, so I left."

Detective Collins tapped his pen on the notepad, scanned his notes, and looked up. "This is when you went alone to the movies and then for your walk?"

I nodded, ignoring the note of suspicion in the way he'd said it.

"And describe what it was like when you came back?"

I squeezed my hands between my thighs to stop the shaking. "She was dead."

I tried to shake the image of Dani lying there, her mouth open. I could have almost believed she was mid-sentence, about to make a witty remark, if not for her reddened skin and the bloody tears in her sweater. When I knelt beside her, my fingers searching for a pulse, I'd noticed it was actually my sweater. Seconds had passed, and my trembling body understood before I could.

My stomach churned, hot liquid rushed through my throat, and the skin around my neck tightened as I relived the moment. "I tried to feel for a pulse," I said. "But there was just so much blood. It looked like she had been stabbed, and she had slits in her skin." I raised my hand to my neck. "It was too late." I sniffed, and tears rolled down my cheeks.

Shelley drew her chair in closer and reached a hand across the table. "What did you do next?" she asked in a soft tone.

Heat rushed to my head. "I threw up. I couldn't breathe. There was all this blood on me." I remembered the sensation of wanting to claw at my skin and fought back tears that laced my lashes. "Then I called the ambulance."

Collins paused and allowed me to take a slip of water. "Did you notice anything different about the room?"

I looked up to find the detective eyeing me closely.

"The window was broken, and it was messier than usual, but I didn't check for anything."

"Does anyone else have access to The Bells?"

"To get into the building, you need a code. It's mainly for the cleaners, and it changes every week. We're not supposed to give it out, but Ainsley sent it out for the party. For our rooms, we all have key passes, but we don't always lock our doors. Dani was always losing her key pass, and we figured we were safe because we have the furthest room. We never thought anything like this would happe…" I trailed off and buried my head in my hands. Anyone could have walked in and killed her. "Wait, tonight she did," I said thoughtfully, sitting up straight. "The door was locked when Ainsley tried to come in."

Collins made a note. "And do you remember if it was locked when you returned?"

I remembered the blood and her cold body first, then I thought back and lowered my head. "No." I sighed. "It was unlocked."

"Was there anything that looked like it could have caused that harm to Dani?"

Tightness spread through my chest as I shook my head.

"Did you see anyone else when you entered the dorm?"

I shook my head.

"And did you have any problems with Dani?"

My head shot up.

Collins's face was passive, as though he hadn't just completely changed the line of questioning.

A hard lump formed in my throat. "We didn't always get along. We had disagreements in the past, but she didn't deserve to die. Not like this."

Collins hummed his agreement. "Did any of those disagreements ever become physical?"

I blinked. He already knew the answer to that. "Yes." He had probably already heard a version of the story from the other housemates he had interviewed. "Last week, she had taken some of my clothes. I tried to pull them off her, and I fell back into a table when I lost my grip. It wasn't really a fight."

"It must have been difficult sharing a space with someone who didn't respect your things."

I stayed silent. It wasn't a question.

"Can you think of anyone who had any problems with her?" He folded up his notebook and dropped his pen. "Anyone who would have a reason to want her dead?"

I took in a deep breath. "I don't know anyone who would have wanted her dead, but Dani wasn't always the easiest person to be around. She ruffled a lot of feathers, and I think maybe she just pushed someone too far."

"Anyone in particular you can think of?"

Five of my housemates sprang to mind. None of them had seemed fazed a few hours ago when Collins escorted me into the common room.

Red cups and empty bottles littered the long oak coffee table. Shelley was stationed in the corner by the pool table, wet with questionable liquids. The rest of my housemates were sitting on the nude sofas in the center of the room. They sat up straighter as we entered. The sandy-brown walls seemed to close in as their eyes leaped between my tear-streaked face and the police officers, waiting for an explanation.

"What's happened?" Raven asked finally. Her hair was split down the middle and gathered into two buns—one electric blue, the other black.

Either Collins hadn't heard or had chosen to ignore her, because he walked over to Shelley and leaned close to whisper something in her ear. Eyes trailed him, and I fell into the sofa beside Bianca. The damp chair pressed against my exposed skin, but I didn't care. Nothing could be worse than the blood.

"Where's Dani?" Bianca asked. She had changed out of her gym clothes. The ends of her green dress were scrunched in her hands. She curled and uncurled a fist, her eyes searching mine, then moved around the room. The other girls looked up, too, noticing for the first time that one of us was missing. Then they turned to me for answers; the unmistakable truth was already on my face and staining my skin.

Detective Collins stepped into the center of the room, capturing everyone's attention as he spoke. "Dani Bishop is dead."

Bianca gasped, covering her mouth with trembling fingers.

Collins towered over us, looking at each face in turn. Bianca cowered on the edge of the sofa, avoiding eye contact. Nia played with her hair, jaw tensed. Martina's fingers tightened against the book on her lap. Raven stifled a yawn, and Ainsley, the last person I knew had seen Dani alive, stared straight at me, something unreadable behind her dark eyes.

Collins's voice snapped me back to the present. "No one you can think of?"

I blinked. The kitchen came back into focus. The two detectives were waiting for an answer.

I pressed my lips together. My gaze fell to the floor. "No."

"Okay." Collins turned to Shelley with a questioning look. She gave a slight shake of the head, and Collins pushed his chair out. "Thank you for your time. I appreciate it. We will be in touch if we have any more questions."

I stood up, eager to leave and wash the blood off myself.

"Oh, Sienna," Collins called.

I spun around, my heart in my mouth.

He slid something across the table. "Here's my card. Give me a call if you remember anything that may help the case."

ABOUT THE AUTHOR

Simbi Feyisara started writing from a young age, uploading incomplete (sorry!) romance stories online. Things took a turn when she committed her first murder—fictionally, of course—and she hasn't looked back since. When she isn't writing twisty YA thrillers, she is procrastinating, usually with tea and biscuits.

9 781917 217026